Broken Silence

Broken Silence

Published by The Nazca Plains Corporation
Las Vegas, Nevada
2006

ISBN: 1-887895-20-5

Published by

The Nazca Plains Corporation ®
4640 Paradise Rd, Suite 141
Las Vegas NV 89109-8000

PUBLISHER'S NOTE
Broken Silence is a work of fiction created wholly by the
author's imagination. All characters are fictional and any
resemblance to any persons living or deceased is purely by
accident. No portion of this book reflects any real person or
events.

Cover Art by Ross Johnston
Editor, Blake Stephens

Dedication

To Patrick, with deep respect

Acknowledgments

As always, books come to publication through the efforts of many peo-ple. This book is the result of many years of living in the leather com-munity. Every person that I have come into contact with has added to the depth of meaning for life, love, and passion. They are too many to mention, and many would rather remain silent.

One particular person deserves more thanks than the rest. My partner, Michael, who, at times must float between lover, friend, spouse, boy, slave, and erstwhile editor. Without his support and inspiration, none of this would have been written.

Broken Silence

Chuck Williams

Contents

Prologue

The night air was cold. Daniel couldn't believe that he was here, out in the middle of nowhere; somewhere in South Carolina, sitting naked in a cabin. He also couldn't believe that he was about to enter one of the most intense leather clubs in existence, at least the most notorious one that he knew about. It had taken several years of networking in leather bars all throughout the country. Finally, he found someone who alluded to a secret organization of leather men that met once a year to receive new members. The process was long and hard. He had to endure a lot of crap to get here. Now, tonight, he sat naked in a cabin, waiting to be called out for the initiation ceremony. It wasn't going to be too hard for him, he was a top, and the club hierarchy accepted him as such. Tops didn't go through the whole week of humiliation. Bottoms had a rougher time during the initiation process. It was all very mysterious. First, there was the phone call telling him where to be and the date that the initiation would take place. When he arrived at the destination airport, he found out that it wasn't going to be quite as easy as just flying somewhere. The fact was that he had to rent a car and follow a map out here into the middle of nowhere. The definitely was not like going to IML.

During the three days that he had been here, he met men from all over the country, and from around the world. Leather men in all shapes and sizes, with one common characteristic—these were men who were very serious edge players. He had seen some of them at work and he was amazed at the level of intensity that their play took on. The ones with the German accents were the harshest. Then there was the almost crazy looking older guy who kept talking to his friends about a certain situation in Pittsburgh and what to do about it. Apparently there was a small leak in the organization's thick wall of security. Their talk scared him, but not enough to make him want to leave. This was his goal.

The knock came loudly. The door opened and he was forced to his knees. A leather hood was placed over his head and tightly secured. His hands were restrained. He was led out into the cold night. As he was walked through the assembled club members, he could feel the heat from the various bonfires that were burning in the camp for the initiation ceremony. After a few minutes, he was thrown to his knees again and the hood was removed. Men in full leather stood before him on a raised platform asking him what he wanted of them. There was no script for him to follow, so he merely said, "To join your ranks."

After that, a group of men encircled him, offering him their cocks to suck. One by one they shoved their members into his mouth, and, after a few minutes, stepped aside and let another of their group do the same. Within minutes they had all finished, and then they started to piss all over him – over his head and down his chest. When they were through, he was led to the cross in the shape of an X and was strapped to its arms. The man who seemed to have authority said, "Now you must prove your loyalty. Each of our thirteen senior members will let you taste their whip. You cannot make a sound, or you will be asked to leave." He felt the lashes of the first flogger, lightly striking his back. Before long, it was no longer lightly caressing his back, but violently hitting him and causing pain. He held back his cries. This was repeated for all thirteen of the higher members of the group. When it was finished, he was dragged away again, back to a cabin. Here, two men who were obviously slaves helped him into the shower. When he was through, they assisted him as he dressed in his black cod piece, black chaps, leather harness, black leather jacket and cap with gloves and boots. They did not utter a word, and he was too scared at this point to say anything to them. When they finished their work they opened the door, and this time he was led back to the center of the group by two men who were dressed remarkably like he was.

The same spokesman appeared before him, "You have passed the test. Your silence during the punishment is meant as a sign of your continued silence about our existence. You may never speak of us to anyone. You may not write down names or addresses, but must memorize them. You must not approach someone who you do not know that you have seen here. If you do so, it will not go well for you. When you find someone that you think may want to enter our ranks, you must contact the man who led you here, and he will determine if you are to ask this man to join us. From here on in, you are a part of us, and we will stand behind you. We will help you, teach you, and supply you with whatever you need to be a part of us. Do you accept these duties and these privileges?"

"Yes, I do," Daniel said, standing before the group. Then he was led to his place on the side and the entire ritual was started again for the next man joining the group. He felt proud, and no longer scared. He belonged. He *was* a leather man. He just wished that he could tell someone back in Columbus about this night and this group. It didn't matter what those old queens back home said, he really *was* into leather—and in a big way to boot. He had forgotten how scary some of these men were and gave in to the heady elation of now being considered a member of the elect. He was finally a brother of the select Dark Knights of St. Germain. It was going to be a good night.

A Boner Book

Broken Silence

Chapter 1

It was Monday. Billy hated Mondays with a passion. He really didn't have any reason to hate them, other than some vestige of a school-boy's hatred of returning to school after the weekend, but hate them he did. Perhaps it was because he loved going out on Sunday nights and usually woke up with a hangover the next morning. Or, perhaps it was because Monday was *the* major cleaning day at the house. Or, maybe it was because he was always alone in the house on Monday mornings. Even if he did pick up someone the night before, he usually had him leave early in the morning. Most of them left without being asked because they had real jobs that entailed being somewhere five days a week at a specific time. In this regard, Billy was lucky. He only worked three days a week to give himself some spending money. He was able to live in this big old restored Victorian mansion in Columbus because his friends let him stay here for free—in return for cleaning, and, at times, cooking.

He really couldn't call Colin, Derek, and Al his friends. They were much more than that, especially Colin. The three of *them* were involved in a very intense, committed relationship. It was one of those wonderful leather relationships that managed to challenge everything that society, even gay society, said about what it means to be involved with another person. They were in love with each other that was certain. It was nice to see three very attractive, hot men in love with each other. And, Billy was glad that, from time to time, he was invited into their sexual play.

Derek was an Episcopal priest, with blond hair and blue eyes that gave him a grown up English choir boy look. Al was Italian, with coal black hair and dark eyes that seem to cover a volcano of sensuality. Colin was the oldest, having just turned forty. Billy hoped that he would look as good as Colin does when it was his turn to reach his fortieth year. Colin was the hottest, at least in Billy's eyes, because of an in-your-face sexuality that just made you hard being around it. While he liked playing with the three of them, he was always happiest when he and Colin got it on alone, together. It was probably because Colin taught him things. The older man taught him not only sexual things, but also how to dress, and how to cook, and a whole lot of other useful things for a gay man in his twenties.

They had only been in Columbus for about a month. The four of them had moved here together after they had all managed to become a part of a sensational murder that made the front pages of Pittsburgh's local paper. Since Derek's occupation as a priest, and Colin's as a high level hospital administrator were definitely in the public eye, they realized that they had to leave. Even though none of them had done anything wrong, it was being publicly tied to a murder that made it difficult for their respective employers to overlook the media exposure. Al had been a Catholic priest, but had left the priesthood to join their three-way marriage, so he tagged along with them as they left. Billy came along, because he liked being with these guys, and because Colin had a special place in his heart for him.

The house was great. It was a big old Victorian with about twenty rooms, spread throughout three full floors and a major basement area. Billy lived on the third floor with his own living room, bathroom, bedroom, and kitchenette/dining area. It was wonderful, and very private, even if he did have to come through the main house to get there. Of course, that didn't bother him, these men were his family now, and he was very comfortable with them.

The area of town was a little quirky. It was down on the old East End. Colin chose the house because of its proximity to Derek's new church, St. Peter's. He thought that Derek would want the option of walking to the church since their last residence was attached to the church in Pittsburgh. This part of Columbus was full of old houses just like theirs, but many had fallen into disrepair. As always, gay men saw the potential, and the bargain of buying a house in an iffy neighborhood, and started bringing the houses back to their former glory. Still, it wasn't 'the' gay neighborhood in Columbus, that was the Short North, all the way across town. That was where Billy worked. The area was filled with bars, restaurants, coffee shops, and, of course, the gay bookstore where Billy worked three days a week.

Monday's, for Billy, were filled with the job of cleaning the house from top to bottom, literally. This was the day that he was responsible for changing all the bed linens, doing the laundry, going to the market, and, finally, preparing dinner. It was quite a bit for a twenty-something gay man, but, since that was all he had to do in order to live in this great house, and get free food, it was quite a bargain.

He was glad that there wasn't a trick from last night to throw out this morning. He needed some quality time alone. Once he got his bearings again, and eased his headache with something from the medicine cabinet, he started his chores. He went downstairs to gather his cleaning things and to walk the puppy, so he wouldn't have to include cleaning up after the puppy along with the rest of his weekly chores.

He made good time, and managed to get the whole house, including the dungeon in the basement cleaned by early afternoon—after all, there were four homosexuals in the house—they tended to be tidy and clean. He picked up the grocery list and went out into the world. It was hard doing the shopping for four men, each with different tastes and different levels of fussiness over what they liked to eat, and what they liked to have in the house to use for snacks.

By early evening, he had put all of the groceries away and had managed to cook what looked to be a very good meal. Mondays were 'family night' at the house—as best they could, all four men had dinner together on that night and spent some non-sexual time together. Colin truly enjoyed these times, and so did Billy.

Derek was the first to arrive home, and it was always difficult for Billy to translate the man that he saw naked from time to time with the man who was standing in the entrance hallway, going through the mail, with the black clothes and starched white collar of a priest.

"Hi Derek, how was your day?" He asked as he came from the kitchen to find out what was causing the puppy to go crazy.

"Fine Billy—a little long. I used to always take Mondays off, but this parish insists that Mondays are the day to visit all of the people that couldn't be in church on Sunday."

"That must be quite a list, Derek, there aren't very many people in church any Sunday," Billy sincerely replied, without one bit of sarcasm in his voice.

"True Billy, but hopefully that will change soon. Has anyone else come home yet?"

"No, you're the first."

Just as he finished answering Derek, Colin and Al arrived at the front door together. Colin had taken a position a little lower than the one he had in Pittsburgh, and didn't have the freedom of leaving early as often as he did in the previous hospital, at least not in the first year. Al was taking graduate classes and teaching at one of the local universities. They didn't usually arrive home at the same time.

When Colin came in, he kissed and hugged Derek, with Al following suite. "Something smells really good," Colin said as he looked at Billy.

"Well, if I'm going to be treated like some Irish housekeeper, and ignored when the Master of the house comes in, I might as well get back to my duties in the kitchen, Sir," Billy responded. But before he could turn and go back down the hall into the kitchen, Colin grabbed him and hugged him, finishing off with a passionate kiss.

"That's better," Billy said as he turned and went off to finish the preparations for dinner.

Soon the entire family was gathered around the table in the oak-paneled dining room. Everyone commented on how good the meal was, and Billy took pride in his work. He had come a long way since that first chance meeting with Colin in the bar, approaching the leather clad older man, asking for some time with the leather top in order to find out what leather and leather sex was all about.

"What's happening, guys?" Billy asked.

"Well, this may be a new city, and a new hospital, but the problems are pretty much the same, at least as far as the hospital goes. Except, they really need some revamping if they are going to stay functional in the next few years," Colin answered first.

"The church is very different, and has very different problems," Derek added. "They are not only unorganized, they are poor as well. I think that there are only about twenty that come with any regularity, most of them gay men. That's ok, but sometimes, I think that coffee hour sub-stitutes for Sunday tea dance. I often see a coupling going on—and furtive departures."

"That's kind of neat, actually, but now I feel old. No one has tried to pick me up," Colin said, laughing.

"Well, you are the Rector's spouse. That would be church-queen suicide, wouldn't it?" Al said.

"Has anyone tried to pick up the number one concubine?" Derek said, joining in their playtime.

"You guys are too much!" Billy added, hoping to end this line of conversation.

"Really, the parish is in quite a mess. It has an endowment that it is slowly being whittled away, and the membership is declining. Then there is the other problem—it's a predominantly gay parish, gay men. That's a little unusual. It also creates a little bit of a problem for the few straight people in the parish," Derek added.

"Well, it's about time that *they* got to feel that way," Al responded, not really believing what he said. "I'm not sure that I should pursue becoming an Episcopal priest, it's kind of a relief not to be dealing with these petty problems, given the nature of what Christianity is all about."

"Is anybody going to ask about my day?" Billy anxiously added.

"OK, Billy, how was your day?" Colin gave in and asked.

"It was really super boring. I hate Mondays—and I have all this work to do. And you guys have to decide on a name for the puppy. The cutest guys in the world come over, go ga-ga over him, and ask me his name, and I just say, the owners haven't decided yet. It's dumb, and it's really not fair to keep calling him puppy."

"All right, but remember, we're a trio here. Three gay men trying to name one dog can be the cause of much deliberation," Derek added.

"What about Faustus?" Al asked.

"How about Machiavelli, he's good at getting what he wants," Colin added.

"May I remind you that its my dog!" Derek was quick to interject, "And, I think that he should have a normal name. One that represents the philosophy and the love of the four people in this house."

"Well then, that would be Finocchio!" Colin answered, giving the dog the Italian name of fennel, and the derogative Italian word for homosexual.

"That's great!" Al said.

"I don't get it," Derek said, looking quite perplexed.

"Finocchio is the Italian word for fennel, and the way that Italians refer to homosexuals, Derek," Colin explained.

"How do you know that?" Derek asked.

"You forget that I studied in Rome for two years while in the seminary?" Colin said, smiling at his lover. "Besides, remember old Mr. Scantalucci back in Pittsburgh? He used to refer to us as the finocchios next door."

At first Derek looked as if he didn't like the name. Then, as he thought about it, the name grew on him. "OK, we can call him Finocchio, but, speaking of him, where is he?"

"He's out in the back yard. He really hates it in the house all the time, and soon it will be getting cold out, and His Little Fucking Majesty certainly won't like it out there then," Billy informed the group.

"Are you somehow resentful of the dog, Billy?" Derek asked.

Before Billy could answer, Colin stepped in to intercede, " No, not resentful, but you know how puppies are. They all vie for the attention of their masters. Billy is no different than Finocchio in that regard," and saying that he placed his hand on Billy's.

"You two make me sick sometime. It was better when you had to sneak out to fuck Billy, now he's here all the time," Derek said, smiling at Billy letting him know that he was probably only kidding.

With the house business-at-hand finished, the naming of the dog, the four men helped Billy clean up the dishes. Al had some homework that night, and papers to grade. Derek had a lot of parish work to finish, and some major report to write for the local bishop. That left Colin and Billy with nothing to do. Derek had been fairly emphatic when he told Colin that he wanted to be left alone for at least three hours.

"Billy, want to walk the dog with me?" Colin asked the cute blond houseboy.

"Sure, it's a great way to meet guys."

"Let's go."

The puppy really wasn't leash-trained, but just knew not to tug on it when Colin was holding the other end. Derek was the only other person in the house that had that much control over the dog. It was as if the dog was establishing his place in the pecking order from dominant to submissive, with him directly under Colin and then Derek. The walk that night was uneventful. There were no cute guys walking around the neighborhood.

"So, Billy, are you going out tonight?" Colin asked.

"Colin, it's Monday, only losers go out on Monday nights."

"Billy, this is Columbus, I'm sure that there are bars where guys are tonight."

"That doesn't mean that they aren't losers. Really Colin, no one *should* go out on a Monday."

"Ummm.......................you want to fool around?"

"Oh man, Colin, I thought that you would never ask. Do you think that Derek or Al would mind?"

"They seem to be occupied with themselves tonight, and a man has needs."

By the time that they got back to the house, Billy's erection was readily apparent through his shorts. They let the dog off the leash, and he went running through the house to greet the other two men. Within a few minutes, Colin and Billy were in the basement, with Billy strapped to the cross, facing the wall. His head was encased in a leather hood, with a blindfold over the eyes and a gag securely snapped over the mouth. Slowly, ever so slowly, Colin began beating Billy's back with the leather thongs of a custom made flogger. As Billy writhed with each lash of the flogger, Colin's erection, and the intensity of the whipping became more evident. When Billy's head was writhing back and forth, Colin stopped, and grabbing the boy's waist, plunged his cock deep into his ass, grabbing the younger man's cock and working it furiously. It didn't take long for Colin to cum, and just as he did, so did Billy.

Colin nuzzled Billy's neck for a few intimate minutes after their climax. Then he undid Billy's bonds, and removed the hood, kissing him deeply. They took a shower together in the basement, and found their way back to Colin's room. Billy picked out a movie to watch and curled up beside Colin, knowing that Derek and Al would soon join them.

Sometimes he just felt like being hemmed in by the three men that formed his family. He felt closer to these guys than he did to any members of his family. It was safe here, and he could always be himself.

Later that night, Al came in, fresh from his shower and dove into the bed beside Colin. They spent a few minutes kissing and holding each other. For a brief moment, it looked like another scene would quickly ensue, but remarkably, it stopped almost as soon as it started. Finally, much later, Derek joined them. There was no place beside his lover, so he had to settle for the outer end, on the other side of Al. That was OK with him, he really liked Al. Soon, the three lovers were caressing and kissing.

"Hey guys, cut it out. It's Monday for heaven's sake, and I am the child here," Billy said.

"You didn't mind the *pater familias*'s dick up your ass earlier, did you?" Derek responded.

"Hey, that was private. But you guys are like my parents on Monday nights, and I don't like to be present when my family 'gets it on'," Billy was quick to add.

Derek only shook his head, incredulous that Billy had these strict rules regarding what was and what was not acceptable behavior. He had a pang of jealousy that Colin was fucking Billy on a regular basis, but then again, it did keep Colin a lot calmer and out of his hair when he needed to get something done. Billy really posed no threat to their relationship; he was only a little trifle that Colin found entertaining. Besides, Derek liked Billy as well, although he would never let anyone know how much he liked the blond younger man.

With the four of them all in the big bed, they soon dissolved into quiet conversation about the day and the upcoming week. The touch of each of them on the other was consoling, and afforded the men a sense of security that was often absent in gay life. With so many men in the house, and three of them in a deeply committed relationship, the pressure was off any two of them. It wasn't long before all of them were drifting off to sleep. Billy usually didn't sleep with the other three men, but tonight seemed to be a special family night for them all. Besides, it felt good to have all of them in bed together. Finocchio was on the floor at the foot of the bed. He had tried unsuccessfully many times to jump up onto the bed with the rest of his pack, but he was still too small to make it. He seemed to comfort himself with the knowledge that he was in the same room and would be there if any one of the men got up for any reason, especially if they went to the kitchen for a snack—which they always shared with him.

Chapter 2

The days and weeks passed as the four men and the one dog settled into life in Columbus. Derek, happy to be in a city that had a vibrant gay community, joined several organizations dealing with a multitude of issues. The subjects ranged from AIDS awareness and prevention to the issues that the transgender community dealt with. This, coupled with his responsibilities at the church, kept him busy, including many evenings. Al, began studying for his doctorate in psychology, while teaching courses in comparative religion. Billy spent a great deal of his time finding himself, and experiencing the variety of bars that Columbus had to offer. Meanwhile, Colin was immersed in establishing his professional reputation at his new hospital. He was also in the process of forming an independent consulting company.

Derek, Colin, and Al hadn't gone out to a bar in quite a long time. Coordinating three schedules was exponentially harder than dealing with only two. Colin was the one who felt that it was important for them to go out from time to time. Derek and Al were perfectly happy to have private little parties at home. Billy, of course, went out often, and with great abandon, sometimes frequenting the leather bars, sometimes the dance bars, and sometimes, the local neighborhood bars that had no real theme.

It was a cold, gray October morning when Colin decided that it was time for the little family to go out again. He was mostly bored at work that day, and at loose ends, hoping that the consulting company that he was starting would take off and he could be free of the regimentation of hospital work. He called Derek and told him to make sure he was rested and ready to go out tonight. He left a similar message on Al's cell phone. When the day finally ended, Colin stopped by the gay bookstore to invite Billy out with them, but the boy already had a date lined up for the evening. Then, on his way home, he stopped to pick up some Chinese food so the three of them could eat, take a nap, and begin the long process of getting ready to go out. It seemed odd to Colin that it used to take so long to go out when he was young. The preparations were endless. Then there was the period of time when going out was rather easy, and the preparations were at a minimum. Now, it seemed that as every year passed, it took longer and longer to get ready to go out. Maybe in his gay old age he was slowing down, or perhaps it was just the inertia of doing something that seemed necessary on some level, but really wasn't.

Colin got home and was greeted enthusiastically by Finocchio. The dog truly loved him, and loved him even more when he arrived home with food in hand. He walked into the kitchen with the dog pensively following behind, hoping that some morsel would drop into his domain. Derek and Al were sitting at the kitchen table, discussing, among other items, what they were going to do for dinner that night.

"Hi guys, at least someone in this house still greets me with gusto," Colin said, setting down the packages of Chinese food.

"Great, you got food. Neither of us wanted to cook tonight, and if we went out, we wouldn't have time for a little nap," Derek said, getting up to give his lover a kiss.

They kissed each other on the lips, each holding onto the other tightly. Colin let his hand slip below Derek's waist and started to tease his cock into an erection. Al got up and joined the two in a group hug and grope.

"How do you always know what we need around here?" Al asked as he broke away from the group and went about getting plates and putting the cartons on the table. Derek went to the refrigerator and got them all beers to drink with their meal.

"It's my special powers as a leather top," Colin answered smiling.

"Oh, not the special powers thing again!" Derek cried in mock horror.

"Well, so much for any sort of submissive protocol tonight, I guess," Colin said to no one in particular while he took the first drink of his beer.

"I'm too tired for that right now," was Derek's only answer.

"What would you like me to do, Sir?" Al interjected.

"You can tell that you're new to this life, Al. It can get old after several years," Derek said, touching Al on the shoulders.

"How did I manage to fall in love with the only gay, bitchy, bottom, Episcopal priest who has become jaded after such a short career in leather?" Colin asked Al ignoring his first lover.

"I was only kidding, Colin," Derek answered. "Besides, you'll get plenty of protocol later, after I've had an opportunity to unwind a little."

"We all need that, actually," Colin replied. "After dinner we should all go to our respective corners and do whatever will help that happen."

After dinner, Derek and Al cleaned up quickly and the three men disappeared in the big old house. Colin volunteered to take Finocchio for a walk that night. He loved walking the dog alone. It gave him much needed time to think—when you're in a house with three other gay men, there isn't a great deal of time for that activity. So, Colin and Finocchio took a leisurely stroll around the neighborhood. Finocchio took his time sniffing at every opportunity, while Colin patiently waited for him.

When he returned home and gave the dog his nightly snack, Colin began the ritual that had become so much a part of his gay life. A long shower followed by the meticulous dressing in leather, each piece perfectly polished and placed on his body with precision and care. By the time that he had placed the last of the black leather accoutrements on, his police gloves and biker cap, he turned to find his two lovers staring at him from the doorway.

"I haven't seen you in leather for a while, Sir. I forgot how hot you look in it," Derek said.

"I thought that you found the 'sir' protocol a little, shall we say, 'over'," Colin chided his lover.

"Yes, Sir. I was wrong, as usual," the boy answered.

"Remember that boy," Colin said to Al, "It's not often that you will find the number one boy admitting that he was wrong."

The men started out that night going to the semi-leather bar in the center of downtown Columbus. It was really a combination of a dance club and leather bar, with a hard-core leather space in the back. The three of them caused quite a few heads to turn when they entered. They had made a few friends since coming to Columbus, and spent a little time talking to them as they came across them in the crowded bar. Derek and Al were not adhering to strict submissive protocol, and Colin didn't seem to mind. Of course, when they went to the 'real' leather bar, the lack of protocol would not be an option.

"How about you guys joining our little leather club?" A hefty man of a certain age was asking Colin. "We do a lot, and a lot for the community."

"Aren't there three leather clubs in Columbus?" Colin asked.

"Yes. But we are the best."

"If there are three leather clubs in this town, what do you all do? I mean, do you guys ever get together for a combined play party or anything?" Colin asked.

"Never together, our play parties are for our members and a few guests. Would you and your boys like to come sometime?"

"Well, I do like to play, and so do the boys. However, I'm a little perplexed by the strict segregation you seem to follow concerning the other clubs," Colin continued.

Both Derek and Al were now standing by their lover offering him the fresh drink that they had obtained. Overhearing the conversation, they knew what was about to happen. Colin didn't hold much store in leather clubs, except as a place to find play partners when he needed them. He finally joined one in Pittsburgh to satisfy Derek's desire to be a member. It was true that it wasn't the most rewarding experience. Derek thought that it would be all camaraderie and a kind of progressive orgy, but that didn't happen. In the end, it turned out to be a lot of backbiting and pettiness. Although Colin never said 'I told you so', Derek knew that Colin's reluctance to join had some merit.

"Well, I don't think that I'm ready for actual membership in a club. I'll tell you what. Invite us to your next play party and we'll see what happens," Colin said, and then, dismissing the man he was talking to, retreated to the comfort of conversation with his two boys. The perplexed leather club member, who had never really told Colin his name, stood staring at the trio, felling very much like he *had* just been dismissed.

After finishing their drinks, Colin took his boys to the more intense leather bar. At least it used to be more intense. Now, in addition to the leather-clad clientele, there were the disco boys, all pumped and cologned, and even a few women. Colin always referred to the disco boys as tourists, and he wasn't as hard on them as other leather men were – he always looked at them as having possibility.

There was a flogging scene going on when the trio entered. A muscular young man was strapped to the St. Andrew's cross in the corner. A very officious top was administering a flogging with the longest flogger Colin had ever seen. The flogger itself seemed to be longer than the top was tall. This meant that a wide empty zone surrounded him to enable him to 'twirl' the flogger in real showmanship style.

This time, Colin went to the bar to get the drinks. As he was standing there with his back to the flogger, the talons of the leather strips managed to hit Colin in the back of his head, dislodging his leather biker cap, causing it to fall to the floor. Derek, truly alarmed, went to retrieve it only to hear his Master bark, "Leave it!" Derek knew that in the few moments that the thongs of that flogger hit his lover's head, Colin had somehow made the transition from a 1990's leather top to an Old Guard Master. Derek backed off, and stood by a confused looking Al.

The top, flogging the half naked muscular man on the cross, turned, and in the space of a few seconds, realized that he had come across a somewhat irritated Old Guard Master. He himself was a little too young to have gone through the training and dark rituals associated with this form of leather. Training and rituals that were shrouded in myth, with no one knowing for sure if they had really happened or not. Still, he was drawn to this form of leather and romanticized about the long training sessions, the rituals involved, and the edge quality to the sexual play that was associated with it. He stopped flogging and went over and, after picking up the cap, apologized to Colin. Colin, silent for a little longer than was comfortable for anyone, finally said, "You know, there's a reason that floggers aren't that long. You discovered it tonight. You goal is to beat the man on the cross with that flogger, and not, I might add, ever to hit another top, especially in the bar."

"I'm sorry, Sir," the man nervously said. He was nervous, not because he was afraid of Colin, or even that he had broken a rule, but because he had offended someone who he admired—admired because of the aura and legend surrounding the Old Guard. "I'll let you use this flogger to flog the slave on the cross, Sir." He said, offering Colin the leather instrument.

"My name is Colin. I assume that you are a top, so, just call me Colin."

"Yes Sir, or er, Colin. My name is Daniel."

"Daniel, you seem to be quite drawn to our lifestyle here. What you may or may not know is that a top's cap is never to be touched in public, and certainly never removed by anyone other than himself."

"I know that Colin. I read it in a book by Larry Townsend or somebody."

"Good, don't let it happen again. And, as for your lounge act here, I would suggest a shorter flogger, no longer than the length of you arm from the shoulder to the tips of your fingers. That should give you the ability to wow the crowd without getting into any sticky situations."

"Colin, the offer still stands—you can flog the guy up on the cross, he's hot," Daniel added, holding the flogger out for Colin to use.

"That he is Daniel, but I don't see a decent flogger to use."

"You can use mine – it cost over $250!"

"Like I said, I don't see a decent flogger around. But, if you really want to make amends, come home with us, and I'll use my flogger for retribution."

Within a few minutes, Colin, Derek, and Al were in the car, driving home, with Daniel and the unidentified man from the cross following them. When they got home, they all followed Derek into the basement.

The dungeon in this house was magnificent. Billy and Colin had spent many hours down there arranging it, and 'decorating' it. There were two St. Andrew's Crosses, and off to the side, a sling. There were bondage tables and benches and a wall with a pegboard holding all sorts of instruments used in this kind of sex play. The floor was painted and had an enamel finish, enabling easy clean up for piss scenes.

Daniel reached out and kissed Colin, who remained stone faced. He didn't move when Daniel's hand grabbed his ample crotch, only commanding, "Boys, get undressed."

Daniel, not used to this type of behavior, started to get undressed as well. Colin chuckled, realizing that Daniel was a little out of his league. This was going to be fun.

Daniel restrained the muscular boy to the cross. He turned, his hard-on sticking straight out, to offer the muscular boy's back to Colin. Colin led Daniel to the other cross and strapped him to its wood.

"What are you doing?" A frightened Daniel asked.

"Getting my retribution," Colin answered.

"I meant that you could flog *him*," Daniel replied, indicating the other man strapped to the cross.

"He didn't knock my hat off, did he?"

With that, Colin chose a soft flogger and began to methodically whip Daniel. When he went to get the next flogger, he turned to Derek and Al and instructed them to be polite to the other guest, and help him feel comfortable. He knew that the three of them would be having a great sucking festival over there. He then returned his attention to Daniel, and continued to beat his back, getting harder and harder with the strokes. At first, Daniel complied, because Colin had lulled him into a false sense of security by teasing him with a softer flogger. Now each blow was harder and harder, and Daniel was yelling and writhing on the cross, telling Colin to let him down immediately.

"Have you ever been flogged?" Colin asked.

"No, I'm a top, you fool. And according to the old rules you shouldn't be doing it to me. Let me down!"

"No."

"Come on, you seem like a nice guy, all I did was knock your hat off."

"Shut up and it will be over before you know it."

"I'm a top, I shouldn't be flogged"

"How can you do to someone else what you don't understand?"

Daniel finally gave up and let Colin have his way. In the end, his back was welted and he was in tears. Colin put down the flogger and approached the cross. He put his hands on the man's back and began to lightly massage the area. No skin had been broken. There were no bruises. He reached around the front and lightly played with Daniel's nipples, kissing him on the mouth and reaching down and stroking his cock. Daniel came as soon as Colin grabbed hold of his cock. When Colin undid his restraints, Daniel fell into his arms, his legs weak from the flogging. They went to a bench. There, Colin held him in his arms and kissed him, bringing him back from the edge of the abyss he had taken him to with the flogging.

Finally, seeing the other three boys working feverishly with each other, he went over, and putting on a condom, fucked the muscular boy roughly while Al fed him his cock and Derek knelt behind Al rimming him. It didn't take long for the scene to end. As soon as it was over, the muscle man rushed out, saying that he lived near by and would walk home.

Colin went over to Daniel and offered for him to spend the night in the guest room, if he wanted.

"Could I spend the night with you guys?"

"Well, the bed is big so you can stay if you want," Colin answered, helping Daniel up. When they got upstairs, everyone was introduced to everyone else.

"Who was that muscle hunk we were playing with?" Al asked.

"I don't know, I just met him tonight and never did get his name," Daniel answered.

The men all started laughing, and eventually formed a unified mass in the bed. That was the way they were discovered the next day when Billy came bounding in to tell them about his night.

"Oh sorry, I didn't know we had company," Billy said, smiling sweetly, as only boys in their twenties can do.

"Billy, this is Daniel," Derek said.

As Daniel reached out to shake Billy's hand, they all started laughing, realizing that this was perhaps too formal a gesture for the situation. Daniel, for his part, couldn't keep his eyes off of Billy, commenting to Colin, "How many boys do you have?"

"Just enough," was Colin's reply.

Chapter 3

It was coincidental that Billy had to return to Pittsburgh for the trial of Brandy Mantune at the same time that Al was going to Italy with his parents for two weeks. Colin and Derek hadn't spent much time alone since Al had arrived. Colin was glad for the quiet that was about to descend upon the house and happy for the time that he and Derek would be able to spend alone. Derek had been a little short with everyone the past few weeks, often clashing with Billy. So much so that Billy had begun to refer to Derek as 'La Malcontenta'. Even Al had started to refer to Derek as *La Malcontenta* when Derek seemed to be particularly upset about something.

Colin had seen it before. Derek would often get frustrated with the way that things were and become a little difficult. Colin had learned, over time, that the only way to deal with it was to let Derek have a little more space, and eventually he would come around.

The first night they were alone found them both in the kitchen, cooking. Colin was always happiest when he and Derek would cook together. It was creative – and the result was always satisfying. As they were cleaning up, Derek asked, "Do you miss Al and Billy?"

"Yes and no. Do you think that you and I can still relate to each other alone?"

"We're going to find out, aren't we?" Was Derek's only reply.

That night they read after dinner and then made love. Not major dungeon sex, or even really hot sex, but the kind of sex that couples need every once in a while to prove that their feelings are still there, without all of the extras that leather couples sometimes put into the act.

"Are we going to have real sex, while the others are gone?" Derek asked.

"Of course, but it is a Monday night, and I thought that we just needed to get off together, alone."

"Do you regret Al being with us?"

"Of course not, we both love him. But it is nice being alone for a little while," Colin cautiously added.

"I'm sorry that I've been a little cranky lately," Derek said, nestled his head on Colin's shoulder.

"You know that Billy has started calling you *La Malcontenta.*"

At first, Derek wanted to get mad, but he could only laugh. The name seemed to fit these past few weeks. It's always hard to start out in a new parish. Oh, it was a fine parish, but it just seemed to be in its death throes. A dying parish with Derek presiding over it like a priest administering the last rites, only waiting to begin the prayers for the commendation of the soul when the final breath was expelled. There was a preponderance of gay men and women in the parish, if you could even refer to a parish with a membership of 50 as having a preponderance of anything. Gay men and women in church can sometimes be a little difficult for the clergy person. They become fussy. Al always laughed and joked that Derek has managed to get himself a church full of church ladies – except there aren't any real 'ladies' in the church. Even the straight women did not, in any way, resemble anything close to those old Episcopal church women that he remembered from his youth. It used to be fun, and now, it seemed just to be a job. Maybe he didn't want to be a priest anymore. What would he become? What would Colin say to this?

The next morning Colin went to work as usual and Derek decided to take the day off. With only 50 parishioners, that wasn't too hard. He spent the day cleaning the house, paying very close attention to the dungeon. He replaced candles, scrubbed the floor, cleaned the leather, and, laid in the sling trying to come up with something new and unusual for Colin that night. That afternoon, he made dinner and prepared for his lover to come home.

The dinner that night was wonderful and the sex was very satisfying. No doubt about it, when Colin put his mind to it, the scene could be hot. They were both sated, on many levels when they went to bed that second night. As amazing as it may sound, it was as if the past several months had never happened, and Colin and Derek were the only people in the relationship. It was a nice change.

"Do you think that we might need a couple of weeks alone every once in a while?" Colin asked.

"I was just thinking the same thing," Derek answered, looking up from the book that he was reading.

"OK, its settled, then we will arrange it every so often."

"Colin?"

"Yes?"

"What would you say if I didn't want to be a priest anymore?"

"I would say, do what ever you want to do, be whatever you want to be."

"Could I be a simple little house husband, who cooks and cleans?"

"Absolutely not! You get so nuts when you don't have something to do!" Colin responded with gusto. Derek smiled, knowing full well that his lover was right.

The rest of the week was spent relaxing in the evening, going to coffee shops and movies. It was like a vacation, except that both of the men were working. By the weekend, Colin suggested that they go out on the town again. To get himself in the mood, Colin went to the basement to get ready. The leather was kept down here anyway, but tonight Colin was dressing in the dungeon, using the sling as a dressing table. He remembered when he and Billy were putting this room together. They were doing it to please Derek. When they hung the sling it was like the center of the house was again installed. Colin had too much religious upbringing not to see the similarity of using the dungeon as a tabernacle in the house. At the same time, it was somehow disconcerting to him, customs that the leather community had adopted would often parallel those of liturgical religion.

They went to several of the bars, with the intention of ending up at the true leather bar by the end of the evening. Unfortunately, at the first bar, Colin's ex-lover, Tony, drunk as always, made a minor scene and they quickly left, not through intimidation but out of a desire to simplify the evening. By the time that they got to the last bar of the evening, they both were bordering on having too much to drink. It was almost a *deje vous* experience – they walked in and a scantily clad muscular man was being flogged by Daniel, only this time, the flogger was much shorter, and Daniel's flogging technique was much less theatrical and a little more intense.

When he noticed Colin, he caught his eye and handed him the flogger. Colin was not one to publicly perform, at least not in this venue, but he started flogging the man on the cross. The victim noticed the change of hands and was startled to find himself *enjoying* what was going on. Colin flogged him for a reasonable time and then let him down from the cross.

"I didn't say he could get down from the cross," Daniel said, half-smiling.

"I don't see a collar on him, and since I'm obviously the senior top here, I made that decision. He's had enough, any more and it won't be enjoyable for him, and it would be just more work for us."

"Let me buy you and Derek a drink," Daniel said, placing his hand tentatively on Colin's shoulder.

"Make it Diet Coke, we've had enough to drink."

"If I made it liquor would I have a chance at topping you like you did me?"

"Well, you could try. But be sure of yourself, I wouldn't want you to fail. The results could be disastrous," Colin responded.

The three men ended up in the dungeon that night with Colin and Daniel taking turns at topping Derek. At one point, Daniel was fucking Derek while Colin was feeding him his cock. They leaned over the sling and started passionately kissing each other, the way that tops do when the scene is really good and there's a hot boy between them. Really, when there are two tops, the passion is definitely between *them*, the boy between them only becomes a conduit.

The next morning Daniel asked where Billy's room was – he wanted to wake him up. He was disappointed when Colin said that Billy was out of town and probably would be for another week. Colin made a mental note to tell Billy that someone was definitely interested in him.

After Daniel left, Colin and Derek decided to blow off the day and just do a lot of nothing—it was Saturday. They went to the gym, out for lunch, and then took a long nap. That night they rented movies and made dinner. It was like old times. They made love that night and awoke the next morning refreshed. Colin went to liturgy at St. Peter's and stayed for coffee hour. Derek had many meetings this afternoon, so Colin was going to be on his own, and he was looking forward to it. When he got back to the house, the phone rang, and a familiar voice merely said, "He wants to see you."

"Where?" Was Colin's only reply.

"St. Joseph's Cathedral, at 3 o'clock. Can you make it?" The mysterious caller asked.

"No problem, I'll be there."

He didn't have much time. He changed into casual clothes and went off the short distance to the Roman Catholic cathedral down the road. He entered the cathedral and was drawn immediately to his former life – the smell of the candles and incense from the morning Masses still lingered among the cold silence elicited by the stones of the building. He blessed himself with holy water, and genuflecting, found a pew. In a few minutes, the familiar figure of his cousin, Dominic, came out from the shadows. Dominic and Colin had grown up together, and were even lovers for a short period of time. But Dominic had gone with his Italian roots and joined a group of men involved in various less than legal activities.

Colin got up and embraced Dominic. "He's over here," Dominic said and led Colin to the sacristy. When the door closed, Dominic was gone and Colin was alone with an older cleric, dressed in the robes of a Cardinal of the Church.

"Colin, how good to see you," the Cardinal said.

"Yes, Your Eminence, it's good to see you as well. It's been a long time," Colin said as he first knelt to kiss the Cardinal's ring and then received his embrace.

"How have you been?" The Cardinal asked.

"Fine, Your Eminence. A little change of venue, but doing fine."

"I heard about the trouble in Pittsburgh. I prayed for you – I hope that it helped."

"I'm sure that it did."

"You would have made a good priest, Colin. Definitely a bishop, perhaps even a Cardinal."

"Perhaps, Your Eminence. But then again, perhaps I've chosen the better half."

"Perhaps you did. Are you ready?"

"Yes," Colin replied.

The old Cardinal placed a purple stole over his shoulders and sat quietly while Colin began the age old ritual that gave him such comfort, "Bless me Father, for I have sinned...."

He told the Cardinal about his relationship, and the way that it had evolved. He spoke of his leaving the Church of Rome and of Al's departure from the priesthood. He spoke of orgies and torturing men while engaging in sex with them. At each phrase, the old Cardinal would look up and ask, "Do you think this is a sin?" And Colin would answer, "No". Only when he came to the part about leaving the church and interfering with Al's priesthood, did Colin answer 'probably'. This was followed by a litany of other sins, anger, drinking too much from time to time, materialism and greed. At the end, Colin said, "For these and all my sins, I am truly sorry."

There was silence in the room for a long time. Then the old man started to speak. "You've told me a lot. You are a man who loves men and have formed a relationship first with one and then with two. You have had sex within and outside of this relationship. You have used means other than the conventional of bringing sexual pleasure to yourself and those with whom you couple. All of this you say you cannot accept as a sin. If you don't think that it is a sin, then I cannot condemn you for sinning. In my heart, although I do not share your particular proclivities, I feel that it isn't a sin either. You talk of enticing a man to leave the priesthood. That also isn't a sin. Colin, you are not God. He calls men to the priesthood and keeps the priest close to Him. For whatever reason, it was this priest's time to move on. God released him. You are not so attractive to pull from God what He continues to want. He moved on with you, and you have given him love and shelter. If that is a sin, then we are all in trouble. You spoke of leaving the church, but you and I both know that you can never leave this church. You can worship elsewhere, you can believe different beliefs, and you can deny our traditions. But you don't leave us – you merely are not visible to us anymore. The man you married is a priest in another faith – what option would you have but to be with him. Even if he weren't a priest, you wanted to fullness with him that required one of you to make an adjustment. You made it – out of love, not hatred. I can't condemn you for that. The rest is part of the human condition, and we all participate in the sinfulness of our faulted nature."

Then raising his hand over Colin, he began the prayer of absolution, "God the Father of mercies, through........."

When it was done they spoke of old times when Colin was in the seminary and the Cardinal was a professor. They spoke of church gossip and who would be the next Pope. They spoke of Dominic and family members. When they had finished their reminiscing, Colin went out into the church. Dominic was no where to be found. He had merely been a messenger boy in this case. Colin would see him again, but only when Dominic decreed it would happen. He went out of the Church into the cold.

The old Cardinal got up and walked into the Church, kneeling in front of the tabernacle. "Why do you let the good ones go, Lord? Why can't we old men who guard your message see that we need to change? How many will we loose, and how many will despair at the thought of loosing you? I'm an old man – answer me, let me know before I go if I'm doing the right thing or the wrong. Let me know if the Church needs to change or am I in need of change." He buried his head in his hands and sobbed like a small child.

As Colin walked toward his car, he looked up at the spire of the cathedral, just as the Angelus bells began to ring. He blessed himself and said the ancient prayer of the Angelus. Then he turned to get his car, and wiped a single tear streaming down his face.

When he got home that afternoon, Derek was already cooking dinner.

"What have you been up to?" He asked Colin.

"I went to confession," his lover answered.

"Yeah right."

And Colin left it at that. Derek, wondering if it was true, was happy that Colin continued to find solace in the ritual of confession.

Chapter 4

When Billy returned from Pittsburgh, he had so much to tell everyone about the trial. It turned out that Brandy actually had confessed, but there was a trial to determine guilt and punishment. He was quickly found guilty but only sentenced to 10 years for involuntary manslaughter of the Ukrainian doctor and only 5 years for threatening Billy's life. His defense was that it was a leather scene, and it was all part of it. As much as Billy protested on the stand, Brandy Mantune still only had to serve 15 years, and would probably get out earlier. That wasn't the big news.

It seems that there is a mysterious man that taught Brandy all about leather sex. Apparently, this man is/was an edge player to the extreme, and the depth of the subject in mind was only a minor complication. Brandy finally admitted his attraction to men on the stand, and said that his marriage was a futile attempt at having a 'normal life'. However, his hatred of himself often was revealed in his brutality to the people he had sex with. He admitted that he wanted to teach them a lesson. But somehow, the fact that he was in a consensual sexual act at the time mitigated his culpability.

"*That* probably wouldn't have had anything to do with the case if it were straight people," Derek commented.

"Or if it were interracial," Colin added.

"But, his wife is leaving him, and he lost the bar, and he's going to jail, that's enough for me," Billy concluded.

"But not for a long time though," said Colin.

"And who is this mysterious man that taught Brandy all that he knows about leather sex?" Derek asked.

"No one knows and the judge didn't really seemed inclined to pursue it further. I was just glad that he got sent to jail. I thought for sure that he would get off somehow and come looking for me, because I was the reason that he got caught in the first place."

"Well, we're glad that you're happy. What did you do in Pittsburgh when you weren't at the court house?" Colin asked.

"Saw old friends, went out a couple of times, but the reporters kept hounding me, asking me all sorts of questions. They even asked about Al.

When will he be back?"

"Probably tomorrow or the next day," Derek answered.

"Do you guys think that I need to find a better job?" Billy asked.

"Why do you ask?" Colin said.

"The lawyers always kept trying to say that I was a drifter, and that I didn't have a regular job and that I was living off of you guys here in Columbus."

"Oh great! That's all we need now. An Episcopal priest and his lover are keeping a young boy," Derek said, getting angry, not with Billy, but at the system that always tended to judge him and his lifestyle.

"Let's just forget it. What's done is done, and there is nothing that we can do that will change the perception that those people have of us. I have spent a great deal of my life standing on the other side of what people considered 'right', and I have found out that you just have to be yourself and not think of what other people perceive you to be. When I was young and decided I was gay, the world looked at me like I was crazy. When I came out and decided that I was really into leather, my gay friends looked at me like I was crazy. You just can't please everybody all of the time," Colin added, trying to defuse the situation, and hoping above all hopes that Derek didn't get into one of his black moods again.

"Still, I think that I should probably find a real job. My parents read what they had to say about me in the paper, and they were really embarrassed."

"Well Billy, you're smart, you have a degree. Find something to do." Derek added in his most priestly voice.

"Oh, by the way, and on a lighter note. There's a guy here who is interested in you," Colin interjected.

"Who?"

"Remember that guy that we brought home from the bar one night that you discovered the next morning?"

"Yeah, he was kind of cute."

"Well, his name is Daniel and he was here again. He wanted to come upstairs and wake you up in the morning."

"Our little family isn't growing again, is it?" Billy asked pensively.

"No, I can honestly say that, unless you settle down with him, he won't be a part of us," Colin answered.

"Don't I get any say in this?" Derek asked.

"Oh no! *La Malcontenta* speaks," Billy said laughing.

Derek hit Billy with a pillow and then started chasing him around the house, threatening to harm him in interesting ways. Finocchio started chasing the two of them, thinking that they had some sort of new game to play. Colin took it all in and merely switched on the television. Boys and puppies could be such a trial at times. He was secretly glad that Al would be back tomorrow. It would make the family complete, and act as a nice buffer between Derek and Billy.

Chapter 5

Daniel couldn't get the memory of sex with Derek and Colin out of his mind. He had lots of sex with lots of men, and been in some very intense S/M scenes, but something about the way that Colin handled himself sexually was so hot. While his attention was definitely on Derek and Al as bottoms, it was Colin that he was sexually *attracted* to. All that Daniel did the past few days was dream about having sex with Colin. In those dreams, he often would let Colin top him totally. He never had found a man that could tie together the cruelty of S/M play with the sensuality and tenderness of a passionate kiss. Most tops that he knew would never permit that kind of intimacy during a sexual scene. With Colin, it just came naturally.

Daniel had to get back on track. These guys didn't go out as frequently as the rest of gay humanity. And there was already three or four of them there, and he couldn't, for the life of him, figure *that* one out. Besides, he had been invited to a leather weekend somewhere in the wilds of West Virginia. He was surprised that he had been asked. It was one of the scary people from the Dark Knights of St. Germain. He was to go somewhere in West Virginia this Friday evening, meet up with his new club brother and go further into the wilderness.

His invitation included a reminder of his vow of secrecy concerning the organization and its members. While these men were really quite hot, this whole secrecy and cloak and dagger mentality was getting to him. Still, he felt like one of the elite whenever he put his new bar vest on with the insignia of the club. It was a simple purple Maltese cross worn on the back left shoulder. It was no more than two inches by two inches. It was easily missed, and most people didn't know what it signified anyway. Still, it made him feel complete as a leather man, and gave him the self esteem to carry himself as a top in his hometown, with all of those tired old queens in their little leather clubs.

When he finally got to the meeting place at a really crappy strip mall, he waited around, wondering how he would know who was here to pick him up. It didn't take all that long, and his worries were unfounded. The man stopped a pick-up truck and signaled for him to throw his gear in the back. Daniel had never seen this man, at least he couldn't ever remember seeing him, but none-the-less this man knew him.

They drove and drove, deeper into the wilderness, all the while exchanging small talk that all gay men use when they meet for the first time. Finally, after driving up a very winding road up a mountain, they reached a gate.

"Would you mind going out and opening that gate, and then closing it after I drive through," the rough man asked.

"No problem," Daniel answered, and jumped out of his seat, relieved to have a couple of minutes to himself.

When he got back into the car, the man said, "From here on in it is strict protocol, and before we get to the group area we'll have to get out and change into our leathers. Remember not to talk to any slaves with a locked collar. If they have a simple collar on, they are the property of the club, and you, as a top, have free reign with them. Be respectful. I know this is your first social encounter with our group, so be a little more on guard than you usually are, if you make a mistake, you will probably be punished."

"WOW! I didn't think that I would need a lesson in how to behave!"

"That's exactly the kind of attitude that I thought you should leave behind. But, don't worry, everyone has it when they come here. It's just that you think you know what it's all about, but we're an intense group. Nothing personal, but you need to find your footing before you do anything."

They stopped and changed into leather and then drove a short distance to an open area with bonfires and torches set about, and several cabins in the clearing. Daniel noticed a couple of naked man hanging from crosses, bleeding from their backs. They had been severely flogged. He had never seen a man marked so much from a flogging – he had always taught himself not to draw blood. Then there was the fact that they were naked and it was quite cold outside. Even though it was a mild fall, and most of the East hadn't experienced the first frost yet, it was still too cold to be out of doors without clothes, especially in the mountains.

There was a man in full leather with a shotgun drooping from one arm. Daniel looked alarmed.

"Don't worry. It's not for people. The smell of the blood sometimes brings bears out—we have to be able to scare them away," his guide told him.

Daniel wasn't sure that he was up for the events that could unfold here. Bleeding was one thing, but leaving men hang out in the cold was another. These guys could die. They walked up to the main cabin and were greeted by some of the men he remembered from his initiation ceremony. Before he knew it, he was seated at a roughly hewn table, eating a gourmet dinner that had been set before him by a naked slave.

While he was eating, the guard that was patrolling with the shotgun entered without his gun. Obviously he had past it on to the next person who was on patrol. He grabbed a collared unlocked slave boy by the hair, threw him over a chair and pulled out his cock and began to roughly fuck the younger man. Daniel didn't know whether he should watch, join in, or wipe his mouth with his napkin. This was definitely a different group, and he wasn't sure that he belonged here. How he wished he was back in Columbus, trolling the bar and landing in the comfort of Colin and Derek's dungeon. He knew that he had to talk to Colin about this, but he didn't know how he could broach the subject, and didn't know if he could trust Colin to keep the confidence.

"Hello, Daniel, how are you?" Asked the familiarly faced man who initiated him into the club.

"Hello, Sir. I'm...er...fine," stammered Daniel.

"It will probably take a little getting used to at first. We go where other leather clubs leave off. I hope that you enjoy yourself."

"I'm sure that I will. I just need to get my bearings. Do you mind if I just kind of watch tonight?"

"Club rules state that you *must* play. We want to see what you're made of. But eat first, rest a little, and then we will start the festivities."

"Sir, I have a question."

"Yes?"

"Those men that are outside.....they could die from exposure, and they're bleeding from the flogging."

"Your question?"

"Shouldn't we bring them in before they suffer some medical complication that could permanently harm them?"

"What all do you know about the men hanging out there?"

"Nothing at all Sir"

"You don't know if they are being punished, if they asked for that treatment, or, if their Masters are just taking them further."

"No Sir, I don't."

"Then maybe you shouldn't comment on it until you know more about it."

Then the man left Daniel's table and disappeared behind a door. Before long, Daniel's gear was retrieved from the truck and brought in by a scantily clad slave boy.

"If you will follow me Sir, I can show you to your quarters," the attractive near-naked boy said.

"Sure, by the way, I'm Daniel."

The boy looked at Daniel liked he had just done something so totally out of place. When they were alone, he said, "Sir, we do not ever use our first names here, especially not a Master and a Slave. We, and I mean the both of us, can get into a lot of trouble for that."

"Thank you. Would you like to spend the night with me?" Daniel asked, thinking that this boy seemed to be the sanest person he had met so far on this trip.

"You don't thank slaves, Sir. And you don't ask. You take. Please Sir, follow the protocol. You don't have to ask. Me talking to you like this could get us both in trouble."

"OK boy. You're sleeping with me tonight."

"I will certainly do that Sir, but there are group activities first. You have every right to take me tonight, unless a stronger Master asks for me. Then you will have to negotiate with him for that right."

The boy showed him his room and left. Daniel had a few minutes. There was a sink in the corner. He went over and ran some water into his hands and splashed his face. "Well, a nice situation you got yourself into this time Daniel. What are we going to do now?" Then he wondered if it was against some protocol, real or imagined, that he was talking to himself.

Before long, a knock came at the door. He was greeted by another Master/Top who grunted, "Come on, the party is beginning."

They walked across the compound to a large barn. He noticed that the two naked men had been taken off the crosses. The barn was warm inside. He couldn't believe the panorama that appeared before him. There were men engaged in every kind of sexual activity, and every kind of torture that he knew. One man was having hooks looped through the skin of his chest and nipples. Another man was getting fisted, roughly. There were men getting pissed on, and, in one corner, men obviously into scat were doing their thing.

There were several St. Andrew's crosses in the barn, and men were being flogged with a variety of apparatuses. Some of the floggers had little metal balls on the end, and those were the ones that seemed to be drawing blood from their victims. Men were writhing in pain, and some of them were begging for the scene to stop, but there was a large sign posted over the door --- NO SAFE WORDS. THE SCENE ENDS WHEN THE MASTER SAYS THAT IT DOES.

All of this was exactly the opposite of what Daniel always thought about consensual S/M sex: safe, sane, and consensual. Obviously, this group didn't believe in those three cardinal rules that were followed in the 'polite' society of S/M outside of this compound. He passed through the night with a kind of shocked participation. At one point that night he watched as a screaming man was bound and had one of his testicles removed. Daniel couldn't believe that he has spent so much time and energy joining this group. In the quiet minutes while he was contemplating this, he began to try to discern some way that he could separate himself from the group. He knew that he had to go to a few of their social events, and not make it look like he was totally freaked out by it, this kind of group didn't like people to join and then disappear.

That night, the slave boy from earlier joined him. Daniel had shown his worth as a leather top by participating in some of the floggings going on in the orgy. The slave boy was his reward. The sex that night was perfunctory, with Daniel only hoping for the morning, and the trip back down the mountain to the safety of his car. Who would have thought that boring old Columbus would look great after something like this?

The next day came and went with little change. There was still play going on, but not with the same intensity as the night before. Mercifully, Daniel saw the man whose testicle had been removed and was happy that he was alive, if not walking a little tenderly. He wondered if it had been his request to have this done. As they were getting ready to leave, a man in his late forties came up to Daniel and his guide.

"Hi, we never got a chance to talk to one another this trip," the man said to Daniel.

"Oh, sorry, I'm Da…….., oh, I forgot, no names," replied Daniel.

"Actually, while we're here you can use them, I'm Ben," he replied.

"Oh, nice to meet you, I'm Daniel."

"Haven't seen you at these gatherings before."

"It was only a couple of months ago that I joined. This was my first event as a full member."

"It's a hot playtime."

"Yes, that it is," replied Daniel, hoping not to sound like he was as disappointed as he was.

"Where are you from?"

"Columbus, Ben, and you?"

"The Washington DC area."

"I go there for MAL every year."

"It brings a lot of visitors to the area."

"Do you go?"

"No, I think that is for amateurs and models."

"The parties can be fun."

"But not quite as fun as ours are."

"Well, they certainly aren't as intense," Daniel replied, hoping to get out of this conversation as quickly as possible.

"A couple of my friends from Pittsburgh have moved to Columbus recently. Maybe you know them," the older man began.

"Oh really, who?"

"One is named Billy, the other one's name, for the life of me I can't remember right now."

Daniel only knew one Billy in Columbus. He wasn't sure if Billy or Colin, Derek or Al were from Pittsburgh, their conversations hadn't reached that level of intimacy yet. He did know that he wasn't about to own up to knowing anyone—at least not to anyone from this group. Besides, he was sure that the young, cute Billy couldn't have any connection with anyone from this group.

"No, sorry, I don't think that I know him," was Daniel's only reply.

"OK, keep in touch. Like to do a scene with you the next time we get together," the older man said, placing his hand on Daniel's shoulder.

"Great, look me up."

Daniel got into the truck with his guide and began the descent to the main highway. In a couple of hours, he was back in his car heading for Columbus. He couldn't wait to get home. When he did, he carefully hung up his leathers and unpacked his gear. Then, after the longest shower that he ever had, he dressed himself simply in jeans and a sweatshirt with tennis shoes and went to a coffee shop, simply to be with people who had a better grasp on what constituted normal. He wondered whether or not he should tell Colin of the weekend, and whether or not he should ask if Billy was from Pittsburgh.

Chapter 6

Al was having a difficult time reconnecting after his trip to Italy with his family. It really wasn't his family's fault; they were great. Nobody said anything, but he just knew that they were disappointed with his decision to leave the priesthood. Colin was being great during this time, and Derek was helpful, but he felt out of sorts with himself and his surroundings. He was glad that Colin had suggested that they start going out on a more regular basis. Maybe being in a crowd of men would pull him back together.

When the three of them made their way into the leather bar that Friday, they caused heads to turn as usual. Colin wondered if it was any one of them that managed to cause this reaction, or if it was the combination of the three of them together that caused all of the attention. He did, however, make a mental note that they were going to have to start taking weekend trips. The crowd in this bar was just as static as the one in Pittsburgh. Bars like this were probably all static, but if you had a circuit that you followed, you would always be surprised by what you saw.

Derek and Al were talking with one of their friends when Daniel came up to Colin.

"Hi Colin, haven't seen you guys out in a while."

"Hey Daniel, good to see you. We haven't been going out much, but I think we'll change that for a while. Although I was thinking that it might not be a bad idea to go to other cities once in a while to see some different faces."

"You could join a leather club and go on their road trips to other bars."

"Well, that is always a possibility, but I think that I'll pass on the club for a while."

"Antisocial?"

"No, just not the club type, besides, Derek and I joined one in Pittsburgh and it got a little old after a while."

If this were a comic strip, a light bulb would have appeared above Daniel's head. So there was a Pittsburgh connection. "You guys are from Pittsburgh?"

"Yeah."

"Even Al and Billy?"

"Yeah."

"Did you decide as a group to emigrate to Columbus?"

"It's a long, and essentially boring story."

"Tell me sometime."

"I will, but not right now. I seem to be loosing my boys."

"One of them is missing."

"Well, Billy is a boy and lives in our house, but he's not one of my boys. I'm not sure where he is," Colin answered smiling. "Do you want me to give him your number? He would probably call you. He thinks that you're hot."

"Of course I want you to give him my number. I can't believe that you haven't done it yet."

"I will, but it's up to him if he wants to call you. I can't force him."

"Colin, I bet you could force that boy to do anything," Daniel said, lightly slapping Colin on the shoulder.

"You're probably right, but I try to limit it. I'll let him know that you're interested. I'm sure that he'll call you."

"Any chance of me coming home with you guys tonight?" Daniel asked.

"No, I think that tonight is family night. We haven't been connecting regularly lately. You know how it is, you get caught up with all of the duties and chores of life, and the next thing you know, sex becomes something to get you off. That works for a while, but then you really have to turn up the heat on the scene."

Daniel mentally winced when Colin talked about turning the heat up on the scene. He wasn't sure that Colin wouldn't be as intense as the men on that mountain in West Virginia, but he was sure that Colin would only go where he had been invited by the bottom, and he was sure that, while it may be as intense as the play on the mountain, he wouldn't be as brutal.

"OK, but don't shut me out completely," Daniel said to Colin.

"I won't. So, now I've used up your valuable cruising time. Go find yourself something for tonight."

Daniel left and Colin turned his attention to Derek and Al. They left shortly after that, returning home to their basement dungeon. The sex that night *was* intense. It went on for hours. When they finally finished, Derek only had a couple of hours to sleep before he had to present himself to his parish as the celebrant of their Sunday morning liturgy.

Needless to say, the liturgy that morning was a little lackluster, from the celebrant's point of view. He was glad when it was over and even happier when coffee hour finally ended. He noticed that Colin and Al left right after the liturgy. He was going to have to lecture them on the necessity of having the rector's spouses present at coffee hour. When he got to the house, they were both soundly asleep. He decided to join them.

At some point that Sunday afternoon, Colin woke up, and retrieving Billy, went to the store to get something to prepare for dinner. While they were navigating their way around the aisles, Colin told Billy that Daniel wanted to get together with him.

"Get together, as in fuck, or get together as in date?" Billy asked.

"I'm not sure. Why don't you call him and ask?"

"Do you mind if I do?"

"Billy, why would I mind, you have dates all the time, and I'm not your lover or anything," Colin responded picking up a bag of potatoes.

"It's just that you and I have a really special relationship and I don't want to do anything to jeopardize it."

"Don't worry, you couldn't"

The two men stopped at the video store, picking up a couple of movies and went home to prepare dinner for all four of them. The rest of the day was spent eating and resting, with movies in between the other two activities. At one point, Billy retired to his room and called Daniel. They arranged a date for the next Friday evening.

That night, in bed after making love, Al finally opened up to Colin and Derek. "Sorry that I have been moping around since my trip."

"That's OK Al, I've been waiting for it," Derek was quick with his response. Colin remained quiet, watching where the conversation was going to go.

"I guess that I was sad, and depressed, and having a major attack of second thoughts."

Colin, putting his arm around Al, said, "Al, it's to be expected. But you haven't done anything monumental or irreversible yet, you can certainly change your mind. We would always remain your friends."

"That's what I really love about you guys. You can be so understanding at times."

"Even me?" Derek asked, with a smile.

"Even you, but no, I don't want to change my mind, or even to go back to the priesthood. It was just the first time that I was away from you guys since this all happened."

"Do we have to keep you with us all the time to keep you gay?" Derek joked.

"Very funny, and the religious right would have a field day with that one. No, you don't, but I may need some time to be alone from time to time."

"That's understandable. We all do," Colin added.

"And I want you two to have some time to yourselves every once in a while. You really are the foundation of this relationship, and I would like my foundation to remain strong and intact."

"Al, if this was the first year or two of our relationship I would agree with you that your presence with us would be a strain. However, at this point, we have worked through a lot of those problems, and I don't think that you could weaken our bond in the least," Derek said.

Colin was surprised. Derek wasn't usually this open and forthcoming with information about the relative strength of their relationship. He was also heartened by Derek's affirmation in his commitment to Colin. Without saying a word, he leaned over and kissed Derek on the mouth.

"But, you may be right. Every once in while, Derek and I may need some time alone. Not a lot of time, and not terribly frequently, but he really is my strength."

"Are we going to burst into a rousing rendition of *The Wind Beneath My Wings*?" Derek asked.

"Well.....it's nice to see that *La Malcontenta* still has it in her," Al said laughing.

"I'm going to kill that little blond catamite!" Derek said, not really being as angry with Billy as he seemed.

"Speaking of the little catamite, how has he been?" Al asked.

"Fine, for the most part. The trial was a bore, and he really isn't too terribly happy with the sentencing of Brandy, but he has accepted it. Apparently the media gave him a hard time about not having a visible means of support, and his family picked up on it. But, he's going to call Daniel and they might go out," Colin said.

"Alleluia! Break out the champagne, get my vestments, I'll sing a *Te Deum*," Derek added. "Finally, he has a chance for a man of his own, and not always using mine."

"Don't you mean ours?" Al added.

"Would you two please leave that boy alone?" Colin interjected. "He has never been a threat to either of you, and he's a joy to have around the house. He's just a little lost from time to time. I wish I had a place like this to have when I was his age."

"You mean, back *before* the word homosexual had been invented?" Derek teased, smiling at his lover.

"Perhaps your right, Derek. *La Malcontenta* may be the wrong term for you. Bitch comes to mind."

If they had been younger, they would have started a pillow fight, or rough housed for a while. But the three of them were so mature and adjusted that they just exchanged verbal barbs for a short time and then fell asleep. Before he fell asleep, Colin realized that he had become too close to Billy. Derek's little comments had grown a little too cutting lately for it not to be bothering him. Colin hoped that this thing with Daniel would work out, that way he could legitimately distance himself from Billy without hurting him.

A Boner Book

Chapter 7

The little family was preparing for Christmas the way that all families do, decorating the house, buying presents and determining the menu for Christmas dinner. It was the first time in their relationship that Derek's parents weren't going to be with them for the holidays. The Wilsons had long ago become friends of Colin's parents, the Morgans. The two sets of parents decided that they had quite enough traditional Christmas festivities in their day, and were going on a cruise together throughout the holiday season. It was leaving on the 18th of December and coming back to port on the 2nd of January. Derek was a little relieved. He wasn't looking forward to explaining the entire story of the murder and their flight to Columbus. Still, there was a little emptiness when he thought of a Christmas without his family. Al and Billy decided to spend the holiday in Columbus with their household family, and Daniel would be joining them. Daniel and Billy were hitting it off famously together. They had dates and dinners. They went out to the bar together and talked for hours on end. As of yet, Billy hadn't had sex with Daniel. He was trying desperately to make this a mature relationship that would work. He resigned himself to beating off a lot, and having sex with Colin, although that was becoming more and more infrequent. He even had a couple of experiences with Colin, Derek and Al. He told Daniel about them so he wouldn't feel like he was cheating on the man that he hoped would soon become his lover.

Christmas dinner this year was to be the five of them, along with a few lost souls from Derek's parish. The holiday dawned on them without much fanfare. The services at the church were, of course, beautiful, or at least as beautiful as they can be with so few people. Colin and Al prepared a wonderful dinner with Billy helping out. Their guests arrived and the dinner party was a success. Still, Derek breathed a sigh of relief when the lost souls finally left for their homes.

The men sat around sharing some Christmas cheer. Al said that it was unusual for him to be in a room with a group of men all of with whom he had sex. That caused a few chuckles between them, and then Daniel noted that he had sex with all but one, the one that he really wanted to have it with. He pulled out another pleasantly wrapped present and handed it to Billy.

"But we've already exchanged presents, Daniel," the young boy protested.

"I know, but this one is special, and it demands a reciprocal present."

Billy accepted the small package and ripped open the wrapping paper. The box contained a leather collar about and inch and a half in thickness that buckled in the back and had a place for a lock to be placed. There was a lock beside the collar in the box. Daniel was nervous that Billy would not accept this present, knowing that the exchange present required the boy to have sex with him. Billy picked up the collar and went over and knelt in front of Daniel, holding the collar out in front of him, offering it to Daniel to put around his neck. When Daniel had secured it, Billy handed him the lock.

"Not yet Billy, let's do the collar thing for a while before we lock it," Daniel said.

As he stood up, Billy quickly looked over to Colin. It was just a split second; he seemed to be begging for approval from the man that he admired. Colin smiled and winked at him, giving him permission to move on. All of this subterfuge was not lost on Derek who knew exactly what was going on. He was watching both Billy and Colin carefully, praying that neither would stop the direction that things were going. He breathed a sigh of relief when Colin smiled his approval.

"Colin, would you mind if we use your basement area tonight? I only have an apartment, and the facilities aren't quite as established there," Daniel asked.

"Not at all, be my guest."

"You sure that you guys don't want to use it tonight, I mean, I wouldn't want to spoil your Christmas sex for you."

"We will definitely have sex tonight, but we have a bedroom, and sometimes sex is even more fun in the bedroom."

"Of course, you all could join in and it could be a regular dungeon party," Daniel added.

"No, not tonight. You two need to do it alone tonight. There will be plenty of time for us all to get together like that in the future," Colin answered, and Derek breathed his second sigh of relief that night.

So, that night, Daniel and Billy consummated their relationship in the basement while Al, Colin, and Derek made love in the spacious bedroom on the second floor. The two scenarios were completely different. The two in the basement did everything that leather men do when they have sex while the three upstairs reveled in each other's bodies the way that only men who are both in love and comfortable with each other could. The end result was the same. The two men downstairs and the three men upstairs all climaxed and ended up holding onto their respective partners. When they were done, Colin and his lovers fell asleep in their bed. When Daniel and Billy were finished, they took a long shower together and then Daniel climbed into Billy's bed with him. They had sex two or three more times before morning. Billy was in his twenties and had been waiting for Daniel for a long time.

The next morning, Derek was the first one up. It was a Saturday, so no one had to go anywhere today. He went into the kitchen and started getting ready to prepare breakfast. He was startled when he heard steps on the back staircase. He was even more startled when he saw Billy. Billy was usually the last one up.

"I expected the bride to sleep in on the morning after her honeymoon," Derek said jokingly.

"I'm just so excited about everything. About being here, and being on my own, away from my family. About spending Christmas with you guys, and about Daniel. He's really great, I hope that I don't fuck it up some way."

"I'm sure that you won't. You've been taught well."

"Derek, I know that you're jealous of what Colin and I do…."

"Not jealous Billy, just a little irritated from time to time. Leather tops, and you will discover this the longer you stay with Daniel, need a little sexual frustration in order for them to keep up the stamina of an extended scene. You took all of Colin's frustration away. In a way, you tamed him. And, we all know that he has a tremendous ability to express himself sexually, but you kind of made that expression for me a little more vanilla that it would normally have been."

"Sorry Derek, I didn't realize that."

"Neither did I at first, and I'm sure that Colin still doesn't realize it. And don't get me wrong, vanilla sex is great and needed from time to time in our relationships. But what really gets me going, and what really keeps me interested, is when Colin can be almost brutal with me. He needs an edge to him."

"I am so sorry Derek, I….."

"You don't have to apologize. I'm just looking forward to the first time that he and I are together after a few days of your new position as the collared boy of another man."

"Can we all have breakfast together?"

"Of course Billy, we can have breakfast. That was my intention."

"Derek?"

"Yes Billy."

"If this works out with Daniel, I'll be so happy, but I really would miss you guys if I moved in with him."

"So, when the time comes, ask him to move in here. You guys can pay rent or something and we can have a little community of our own."

"Do you mean that?"

"Yes, but I'll have to check it out with Al and Colin of course. Now, let's get this breakfast started."

By the time that they had prepared breakfast, the other men were up and in the kitchen. The five of them talked like they had always been together. There was a great sense of ease among them. Daniel and Billy made plans to go out to a bar that night to publicly celebrate their coming together. They tried to convince Derek, Colin and Al to come along and make it a bar party. Colin steadfastly refused. He had plans that night for Derek and Al that involved the dungeon. Al really wasn't sure why Colin was refusing to go out, he loved to go out. Derek had a clue that it had something to do with getting that leather edge back with his lovers.

Chapter 8

Derek was having one of those horrible Monday mornings that clergy all over the world hated. He thought that if the phone would ring one more time, he would simply loose it. But ring it did.

"St. Peter's!"

"Well, that doesn't sound too friendly and inviting," Millicent, a voice from his past said. The Reverend Millicent Barclay had been his curate in the parish in Pittsburgh. She had gone through a particularly difficult divorce during his tenure there.

"Oh Millicent, sorry about that. It's been one of those days and I thought that you were just another person needing something right away. How have you been?"

"I've been fine, Derek. How have you been? How's Columbus and how is everyone in your growing little family?"

"Columbus, the city, is great. Colin is fine, so is Al. Billy is Billy, but he's just fallen in love. The parish is a little rough around the edges, and not so healthy, but, otherwise, life is great."

"You'll never guess what!" Millicent almost shouted into the phone.

"I bet I couldn't," was Derek's only viable response at this point.

"You remember that article I wrote about being a priest and getting a divorce?"

"Yes, somewhat," Derek replied wishing that he would have really read the article instead of skimming it.

"They asked me to write a book about it, and I did. And, it's going to be published."

"WOW! That's great."

"But that's not all," Millicent said, leading him on with a gay man's sense of suspense.

"They're making it into a movie?"

"No, silly. But someone in your diocese is asking questions about me becoming your next bishop."

Derek had to stop and think a minute. He wasn't sure how he felt about this. Of course he was happy; he truly loved Millicent. On the other hand, he was once her boss, and if she did get ordained as his bishop she would be *his* boss, but in a bigger way. A much bigger way. In the few minutes of stunned silence that he allowed himself, he mulled these issues over along with the nagging pettiness of thinking that she gets a divorce and becomes a bishop, he is remotely linked to a gay murder case and he is banished.

"Millicent, that's wonderful. Who else is being picked for the short or long list?"

"I'm not sure, it's too preliminary yet."

"And, what is happening to Bishop Bialistock?"

"He's retiring, I think, but not for a couple of years, so this is way preliminary."

"Have you had any interviews yet?"

"Just a few. They have been somewhat unofficial so far. I'm not really too sure of the process, I never thought that it would matter too much for me."

"This is great, are you coming to Columbus any time soon?"

"I'm here right now, and was calling to see if you could meet for lunch."

Derek, while being very fond of Millicent, wished that there were some way possible for him not to meet her at this very moment. He had to digest the information that he had just received. However, feeling that tug of good old English sense of duty, he replied, "Sure, when and where?"

"Do you know the short North?"

"Do I know the short north? Of course I know the short north. How about we meet at the coffee shop on the corner."

"OK, about 11:30?" Millicent asked.

"That will be fine, see you then."

"OK, later."

Derek rustled though the papers on his desk, made some calls, and cleared his schedule for the afternoon. He really wanted to share the news with Colin and also share his feelings. Then he felt a pang of guilt because he didn't think of Al to share the information with; but Colin knew him a lot longer, and probably understood him better than Al did. He called Colin's office but he was in meetings in another building for the better part of the day.

The morning passed by quickly and Derek finally went off to meet Millicent. They had a great time. It was so good of a time that lunch lasted for over three hours. He really missed his relationship with a coworker that could offer him suggestions on how to run the parish, and someone with whom he could joke about the parishioners without feeling guilty. Around the middle of the afternoon it was apparent that Millicent couldn't stay much longer, but had to get ready for one of her interviews, and then was on to another city in Ohio for further investigation. They bid each other good bye on the street, both of them stunning in their clerical collars.

Derek decided that he would not go back to the office but go home a little early. When he got there he was greeted with Finocchio's jumping and barking and Billy's struggle with a cookbook and a can of cream of tartar.

"What are you doing home so early on a Monday afternoon?" Billy asked, looking up from his cookbook.

"I decided to call it an early day and get some rest before Colin and Al come home tonight."

"Want to give me a few pointers on this recipe?"

"Sure, but don't you have a date with Daniel tonight?"

"We're meeting for drinks a little later."

"You guys see each other every day?"

"Yeah, it's getting pretty serious. We're almost ready for that moving in stage."

"Have you made any decisions about where you two want to live?"

"We haven't talked about it yet, but I really would like to stay here. I hope that he cool with that and that the offer still stands with you guys."

"Let's all talk it over dinner tonight. Now let me see your recipe. I've got to get some rest." Derek helped Billy with the sauce that he was trying to make. Then he went upstairs and climbed into bed with the dog and fell quickly asleep. He didn't hear Colin or Al come home and didn't even smell the dinner cooking. Finally, after calling for him repeatedly, Colin came upstairs and gently woke him with a shake.

"Hey, little one, are you OK?" Colin asked, studying his lover's face to determine if there was any thing physically wrong with him.

"I think so. I'm just really tired."

"You're breath smells like you had one of those four martini lunches."

"Well, not quite four, but yes, I met Millicent for lunch today."

"Oh really, that's great. How's she doing? Why didn't you invite her to dinner tonight?"

"She had to go to Cincinnati for a meeting. She's doing well. As a matter of fact, she wrote an article that got a lot of praise in church circles, and it turned into a book."

"That's great, with her luck, it will be made into a movie or at least a Lifetime TV mini-series."

"I almost said that same exact thing, but, no it's not. *But*. . . she is being considered to become the bishop of this diocese."

Colin had to compose himself for a minute. He was still a little unused to women as bishops, and his relationship with Millicent was far from stellar. "That's wonderful, are you happy about that?"

"I'm not sure. I thought that I would be and then I felt a little, I don't know....slighted."

"Perhaps it's just a little professional jealousy," Colin said patting his lover's hand.

"Yeah, that and a little feeling like there will never be an openly gay bishop in the Episcopal church."

"I understand. Do you want to stay up here and talk about it for a while? We can let Al and Billy start on whatever Billy's culinary masterpiece is tonight."

"Well, I would like to talk, but not right now. I need time to think of how I really feel about this. Let's just go to dinner with the boys."

"Derek?"

"Yes?"

"I love you."

"Thanks, Colin, I needed that right now. I love you too. Let's join the rest of the family."

When Derek got out of bed, he seemed a little unsteady. Colin quickly assessed his lover's condition and decided not to ask him again if there was anything wrong. Perhaps he was just tired, or had too much conviviality at lunch. In a couple of days he would ask Derek when was the last time that he went to the doctor's. Derek hated it when Colin became motherly about his HIV status.

They joined Al, Billy and Finocchio for dinner. The dinner that night was perfect, Billy was coming along nicely as a gay man who could cook. They even had crème brulee for desert. As they were lingering over coffee, Derek turned to Billy and said, "Don't you have something to ask Colin?"

"I thought that you were going to ask him," Billy said, looking as nervous as possible for a twenty something gorgeous gay man.

"No, that's up to you."

"OK, enough. What are you supposed to ask me, Billy and/or Derek?" Colin finally said.

"Well, Daniel and I are getting along really well, and, we think that we would like to move in together and I really like living here. And, well, I guess I was just wondering if he could move in with me upstairs."

"Billy, I'm glad that you guys are getting closer. But, I'm not the only person in the house; there are two other men to consider here. I think that it should be a joint decision. Not only me, but Al and Derek as well," Colin said, hoping above all hopes that the other two men would be agreeable to the arrangement. He was genuinely fond of Billy and didn't want to have him move out, even though they had stopped having sex when Daniel came into the picture, at least after Daniel and Billy became a serious item.

"I'm OK with it Colin," Derek said.

"Me too," added Al.

"Are you sure?" Colin said looking closely at Derek. He knew that Billy and Derek could go at each other from time to time and that Derek had little patience for Billy and his youthfulness.

"Really, it's OK, Colin," replied Derek.

"Look Colin, if it's a problem for you, Daniel and I can move into his apartment," Billy interjected thinking that Colin wanted him out of the house and was trying to coax Derek into saying it.

"That's not it at all, Billy. I would be happy for the two of you to be here. What does Daniel think about it?"

"He doesn't know yet."

The three other men at the table started to laugh. It was just like a twenty something boy to plan a future for the man he loves without including him in on it first. Billy didn't see what was so funny; he was just relieved that he could stay with his friends.

"I'm going to tell him later tonight. I just wanted to check it out with you first," Billy added, trying to justify his actions.

"That's understandable. Tell him we would love to have him here," Colin said.

"And we would pay rent and everything, and I could still do the Monday chores and it will be great," Billy said, getting up to clear the table.

That night he did tell Daniel who seemed quite agreeable to the idea of moving in with them. They spent the night at Daniel's apartment, having sex and talking all night about what they would do, and how they would put Daniel's stuff in Billy's space. It wasn't going to be that hard; Billy didn't have much anyway.

Chapter 9

The next evening, Daniel found himself alone for the night for the first time since Christmas. Billy said that he had things to do and Daniel welcomed the break. He had never lived with anyone, and moving in with four other guys and a dog right off the bat was going to be a real transition. But, he really liked Billy, not to mention the others. And Colin still had the ability to give him an erection when he thought about sex with him. He wondered if that was going to be a possibility once he moved in. They were leather guys, so Daniel was sure that they would at least have the occasional dungeon party, and he thought that he would surely be invited. When the phone rang, he thought that it would be Billy calling to report in for the evening.

"Hello, Daniel?" Said the voice on the other end.

"Yes?"

"This is Ben."

Daniel's silence on the other end gave Ben a clue that Daniel didn't remember who he was. "Ben, from the Knights of St. Germain. We met at a play party in West Virginia a few months back."

"Oh right, sorry. A lot has happened since then," Daniel said, wishing that he hadn't answered the phone. He really regretted that he joined that club and was hoping that they would just go away and leave him alone.

"We're having a little play party again. This one is going to be in Georgia. We expect you there next month for it."

"Ben, I would really love to do that, but I've met someone and it's getting serious. This wouldn't be a good time to leave for a play party."

"Congratulations. I'm happy for you."

"Yeah, it's a guy that I met right after I joined the club. He's really great and it has taken us a long time to get it together. We're moving in with each other in a couple of weeks."

"Like I said, that's really great and I'm very happy for you. Is he into leather?"

"Yes, he is."

"Well, after you two have been together for a while, you'll have to bring him to a club function to introduce him. If we like him, maybe he'll become a member."

"I'll be sure to bring that up when the time comes," Daniel answered, knowing full well that he wasn't going to subject Billy to these guys.

"But, back to the business at hand, we still have that play party next month."

"I just can't Ben, it's a really bad time."

For a few moments, there was silence on the other end of the phone. Then Ben, obviously choosing his words very carefully, said, "Daniel, these parties aren't optional during your first year. They are required. You have to be there."

"Ben, come on. Tell me that people don't have obligations that could make them absent from a couple of these meetings."

"During the first year, you are at the command of the club. We ask for your presence at these things to make sure that you know all about us and we can show you how to progress in leather."

"Ben, maybe it was a mistake that I joined. Maybe I need some time to rethink this. Is there the ability to take a leave of absence or anything for this?"

"Daniel, I'm a little disappointed. We don't usually let people join our ranks who are indecisive. It won't go well for you, I know that."

"Ben, that's the third time that I have heard this cryptic 'it won't go well for you' thing. What exactly do you mean by this?"

"I'm not really at liberty to discuss that with you, since you are in your first year with us and are obviously having a difficult time living up to your obligations."

The tone in Ben's voice sent a shudder though Daniel. He remembered the men hanging naked from the crosses, their backs bleeding, in the cold. He remembered the screams of the guy having the testicle removed. He really was quite scared and didn't know exactly what he should do. After a few minutes of silence, he decided that he could probably play their game the first year, then drift into the background.

"Ben, maybe you're right. Maybe I should be at the play party next month. I'm sorry, it's just been a rough couple of months. Give me the details."

"I'm glad that you reconsidered, Daniel. The details will be called to you when the time comes. Make your reservations to fly the second Friday of the month, you will return on Sunday or Monday, depending on your preference."

"Thanks, Ben. I guess that I needed a little reminding of my obligations," Daniel said, lying through his teeth.

"Good night, Daniel."

"Good night."

As soon as he hung up the phone, Ben dialed another number. A gruff voice answered. Ben related the conversation that he just had with Daniel, indicating that maybe a mistake was made in asking him to join the club.

"Have you dealt with the other matter, the Pittsburgh thing?" The gruff voice asked.

"I'm still trying to track him down. I know that he moved to Columbus, but didn't want to do anything too visible in trying to find him. I think that Daniel can help us with this, he goes to the bars there and will probably run into him."

"We need to teach that boy a lesson," the gruff voice said.

"Shouldn't we teach that top and his priest boy a lesson as well, he's the one that actually caused the trouble?" Ben asked.

"From my understanding, the top is fucking the boy on a regular basis. By teaching the boy a lesson, we will certainly send a message to the other two."

"And Brandy?" Ben asked.

"We'll take care of him later."

"I don't want any of this to come back to haunt me. You know that I was present when Brandy did his thing. I had no idea that he would be so stupid as to get caught."

"The authorities should leave us alone. We are a society to ourselves, and we have our own rules and customs," the gruff voice said.

"Sometimes I think that we go too far in our get-togethers and in our play."

"Perhaps, but that's our business. Besides, how many people have died during our scenes? It's only been a handful. I'm sure that inept tops cause that many deaths every year, and we never hear about it."

The two men hung up shortly after that. Meanwhile, back in Columbus, Daniel was stewing about the whole thing. On the one hand, he was becoming frantic at the thought of having to subject himself to this group, then outright terror at the thought of what they could do to him. He really needed to talk to someone about it. He just couldn't bring Billy into this; for one thing, he was young, and that means that he loves to talk to everybody about everything. Maybe Daniel could confide in Colin. After all, in a couple of weeks they will be living together. Colin seemed to have a good handle on his life and probably already knew about this leather group. He would know the right thing to do. And, once he told him how to deal with the club, maybe he could give him a clue as to how to tell Billy about it. Daniel just knew that, at this stage in their relationship, Billy wasn't ready to have Daniel go off by himself for an orgy somewhere in Atlanta. That was another thing, who was he kidding? One thing Daniel was really sure of – he would probably be flying to Atlanta, but he was sure that he would have to drive somewhere out into the wilderness. With his luck, he'll survive the scrutiny of the leather club only to be consumed by kudzu in the woods. That *was* the way his luck seemed to be going these days.

While Daniel was wrestling with his demons, Colin and Billy were having a heart to heart in their basement. This time they weren't in the dungeon, but in the laundry room sorting and folding clean laundry.

"Colin, I'm going to miss having sex with you. It's not that I don't want to, but I think that I should concentrate on Daniel for a while," the younger boy said.

"Billy, that's quite all right. Remember, I have two lovers of my own right now, and this will give me a chance to get back on track with them."

"I know, that was what Derek had said."

"You and Derek discussed this?" Colin asked incredulously.

"Yeah. Although he never said it to us, I think that he was jealous of what we did."

"Wow! I never thought that he got jealous about me at all," Colin said, realizing that even though he knew his lover through and through, there was still that magical area of mystery that everyone keeps to himself. When it came to Derek, Colin respected the boundaries of that area.

"But, you could join Daniel and I when we come down here?"

"Yes, and I'm sure that I will, along with Derek and Al. But that will happen when the time is right, and it's just not right yet. You two need to have a little time alone for a while. Besides, I think that I intimidate Daniel."

"You don't have to think. You do. And from what I hear, you actually set out to do it from the first minute of your meeting," Billy said, exchanging a knowing smile with Colin.

"You had to be there Billy. It was a special situation. And, I gave to Daniel what I thought that he needed."

"Are you saying that my wonderful lover and top is really a bottom?"

"No, I'm saying that he is a top. But every once in a while, a top can be so turned on by another top that he is willing to bottom for him. Sometimes that scares him. Sometimes it just shows him that there is another area of his life that can give him some pleasure."

The two men finished folding the laundry and each went upstairs to their respective rooms. Colin found Derek and Al in bed, each reading something that seemed so terribly academic. "Are you guys OK with Daniel moving in with us?"

"Of course, at least that little scamp will have someone to pork him on a regular basis," Derek replied without looking up.

"I'm really OK with it, but you guys realize that you never really asked me before telling Billy that he can move in," Al added.

Colin and Derek were stunned. They both remembered the dinner conversation when Al was asked his opinion right after Colin found out about the planned arrangement. They really both thought that Al was so easy going that he wouldn't mind anything. Once they composed themselves they said, almost in unison, "We're sorry, we just assumed........"

Al cut them off, "It's really OK. I just felt a pang of remorse—feeling like I didn't matter. Then I told myself that I was in a leather relationship and I was third down so I should just keep my mouth shut and do what I'm told. It just seemed like it had already been worked out, that's all."

Derek remained silent. Colin looked at Al for a long time, choosing his words before speaking. "Al, I don't think that we have reached that level of intensity in this relationship, and I don't think that we ever will. Derek is subservient when it really counts, but he also speaks his mind as well. You always have a say in what we do around here, we were just kind of not thinking when we assumed that you didn't mind. Besides, you said that you didn't mind at dinner. Al, you found out the same time that I did."

"I guess that I know that now. I was just thinking that you all had talked about it and then just staged it for my cursory approval. I'm just being a little self-conscious these days. It's the leaving the priesthood thing."

"I know how you feel Al, we're here for you when you need it," Derek joined in.

"I know what I really need tonight......" Al finally added.

Before anyone could say another word they became a writhing mass of man flesh, making love with each other, with Colin clearly in charge of what was going on. They took their time and spent the better part of two hours bringing each other to the edge of a climax and holding off. When they were finished, they were truly spent, in every aspect. As they were cuddling together, and about to drift off to sleep, Colin asked Derek, "Did you really mind what I did with Billy?"

"I guess that I started to after a while."

"Why didn't you say something?"

"Because you would have stopped, and I shouldn't have that right in this relationship."

"Do you think for a minute that I wouldn't stop you if the situation were reversed?"

"That *is* your right."

After a couple of minutes, Colin and Derek said together, "Al, did it...."

"I'm OK, really! Stop it and go to sleep!" And they did just that. All of them fell asleep quickly. Billy was upstairs watching television and wondering if he was doing the right thing with Daniel, and if it was really a good idea to move him into the house. He was just going to have to play it by ear.

Chapter 10

Bishop Bialistock sat at his desk fumbling with some pens. Millicent sat directly across from him, answering his many questions. It was obvious that he had something to say to her and was taking a circuitous route to actually verbalize it. Finally, after a very uncomfortable pause, he said, "Millicent, I'm going to confide in you. I'm actually looking to retire much earlier than every one is saying."

"Bishop, are you well?"

"Yes, I'm doing fine. Of course I'm getting a little old, I'm in my sixties. But there are a couple of other issues and I'll let you in on what they are. Our youngest son has AIDS and isn't doing well. I want to spend some time with him and with my wife. I've pretty much ignored her since becoming bishop and now it's time to pay the bill."

"Bishop, aren't there new drugs for your son?"

"That there are, but they aren't working well, and his liver is giving out. It won't be tomorrow, but I think that I have to face the grim fact that I will be burying my son."

"I'm so sorry. Is there anything that I can do?"

"Well, that's why we're having this conversation. Usually we aren't so open with the candidates for consecration, but these are special circumstances. Again, we usually consecrate who is called, and that person works with me for a while, getting the hang of things."

"Yes Bishop?"

"Well Millicent, the reason that we are talking is that you will surely win the vote. There won't be a lot of time for you to preside with me and get the hang of things. Of course, I will be available for counsel."

Millicent's head was spinning. She knew that she was being considered, but some quirk of human nature had convinced her that she would never become a bishop. She really couldn't believe that this was happening.

"Millicent?" Bishop Bialistock said, interrupting her internal turmoil.

"Sorry Bishop, I guess it just hit me. I never thought that I would become a bishop, and I certainly didn't think that it would be so soon."

"The vote will take place tomorrow. I'm sure that you will have the majority. Will you accept?"

She stared into his face for a moment. She was excited, and conflicted, and worried. Finally, she answered, "Yes." At the time, she didn't realize it, but she never even considered a short prayer before making that answer. As a matter of fact, God seemed to be far removed from these proceedings. This is something that she would remember much later on and something that would eventually lead her to humility.

The next day the vote was taken. She won the majority and accepted the position. She thought that she would find Derek there. He wasn't. She forgot about him for the moment and went with the flow of excited congratulations. Of course, as in every human endeavor, there was the old guard contingent that found it difficult to accept a woman as a priest and, to them, the thought that a woman could be a bishop was just incomprehensible. After making the usual small talk with all who congratulated her, she finally left to spend some time with herself. That evening she finally calmed down enough to call her old friend and boss.

"Hello," a voice answered. It was a voice Millicent didn't recognize.

"Is this the residence of Derek Wilson?" She asked.

This took Al a little aback. No one had ever referred to the house as the individual residence of any one of them. "Yes, Derek lives here. Who may I ask is calling?"

"This is Millicent Barclay, and who is this?"

"My name is Al. Hold on a minute."

Al went and pried Derek away from a book he was reading in the library. Derek knew what Millicent was going to tell him and, as much as he liked her, he just didn't want to hear it. He was having enough problems with the fact that he didn't think that he wished to continue functioning as a priest. Accepting her as a bishop would just be another bitter pill to swallow and he didn't know why he considered it as such.

"Hello Millicent."

"Hi Derek. Guess what! I'm the new bishop!"

"Well congratulations. I had no doubt that you would be making this call."

"Thank you for your confidence Derek. You always had a higher opinion of me than I did."

"When is the consecration going to occur?"

"I assume very quickly, the Bishop wishes to retire as soon as possible. Of course, there will be a committee to plan that. I want you to take an active role in it."

"I'm not so sure that I should Millicent. Remember, I'm a marked man now. At least in some circles."

"Perhaps you're right Derek. But you will come?"

Derek felt that his old friend had perhaps withdrawn her request a little too quickly. However, he couldn't blame her. He wasn't exactly an asset to a new bishop. "Of course, I'll come, and I'll bring the whole family with me."

There was only a momentary pause, but Derek felt he heard a quick intake of air on Millicent's part before she replied, "Great, I'll keep you updated."

"Well, Millicent, congratulations again. I'm very happy for you."

"Thanks Derek, you were very helpful to me when I needed it. I won't forget it. But I really should be going – I'm sure that I have ten thousand meetings I haven't planned for."

"Good bye Millicent."

"Bye Derek."

When he hung up the phone, he remained alone for a few minutes. Strange, his lover, or now lovers, always helped when he had mixed feelings about something. This time he really didn't know how he was going to tell them. More specifically, he didn't know how he was going to explain the feelings that he had at this moment. But, when you're in a marriage, no matter how unconventional that marriage is, secrets can't be kept for long. People who know you intimately know when something is bothering you. Colin had always been very sensitive to Derek's moods, and gave his a great deal of leeway. There was a point however, when Colin would sit him down and demand to know what was wrong. The funny thing was, Colin usually knew what had been bothering Derek all the time. He was just giving his lover a little time to deal with it before making it public.

He went back to the library to find both Al and Colin intertwined on the couch, each reading their own book. When Colin looked up, he smiled, opened up his arm as an invitation and pulled Derek into their embrace.

"I assume that Millicent is the new bishop?" Colin asked as he rubbed his lover's head.

"Yes, she is. Well, she really deserves it...."

Before he could finish, Colin stopped him, "No need to talk about it right now little one. I'm sure that you are full of mixed emotions. We can talk when you're ready."

Derek was thankful for that. He would have just rambled on, making a fool of himself and becoming more confused as he tried to explain what he was feeling. Besides, with Al in his own turmoil right now, it wasn't fair to inject another crisis, at least not one that was the simple result of a little jealousy.

Al got up to take a shower. After he left, Derek knelt down on the floor in front of Colin, pulled his pants down, and started to suck his cock. It wasn't long before Colin came. A man on his knees always got him going quickly. When it was over, he pulled Derek back up on the couch and held him tightly. Neither man had to say anything about what had just happened. They both knew that, at that moment, Derek needed desperately to show his submission to another man. Colin knew this was how Derek was managing to hold onto his identity, almost to confirm the decision he had made a long time ago to be a gay man, and to be a leather bottom. That affirmation seemed to calm Derek.

As they were preparing for bed, Derek reflected on what had just happened. When he was his most vulnerable, he didn't pray. He turned to his lover for sex. Perhaps he really shouldn't be a priest. He really wanted to talk about it now, especially with Al, but he just knew that it would destroy the moment. He knew that tomorrow, he would pray. That was the way that it always was with him, when things calmed down, he returned to his old self and did the things that you were supposed to do. In the anxiety of the moment, he turned to his lover for help. What would he do if he wasn't a priest? He had no idea. The only thing that he was sure of was that Colin would stand beside him. He hoped that Al would as well, but they simply didn't have the same history.

Chapter 11

Moving day for Daniel came not too long before he was to go to the next meeting of his secret leather club. Derek, Colin, Al and Billy all helped so it didn't require a whole lot of time. The only problem that they had was carting all of his things up to the third floor of that big old house. Billy couldn't be happier, but Daniel seemed a little preoccupied to the group. They all assumed that it was because he was loosing some of his independence. They had no idea that he was dreading his next trip—dreading on two levels, he simply didn't want to be with those people and he didn't want to lie to Billy about it. He just didn't know if he should tell Billy about it, risking a fight so early in the relationship, and wondering if Billy would be able to keep quiet about it to other gay men.

They all went out to a restaurant that night. It was an upscale gay place and they had plenty to eat and plenty to drink. Luckily it wasn't far from their home so the drive wasn't going to be particularly bad. Derek and Al went upstairs and fell across the bed. Even Billy was a little tired and drunk. Colin and Daniel stayed downstairs, raiding the refrigerator for something non-alcoholic to drink. Daniel thought that this might be the best time to broach the subject with his newfound mentor in the leather world.

"Colin, I need some advice."

"Well, I don't usually give out this kind of advice, but you should be gentle with him at first, not too rough. Newly married couples need time to adjust, and the wife is sometimes......"

"Not that kind of advice. Would you please be serious for a minute?"

"Ummm. It's going to take a little getting used to with another top in the house. People don't usually yell at me," Colin replied, smiling all the time so Daniel knew that he was only kidding.

"Any way, I joined this really intense leather club a while back and they are giving me problems."

"An intense leather club in this town! That's amazing! I didn't think that they existed. But, my advice is, if it bothers you, just quit the club

Daniel."

"No, it's not from this town. It's kind of international, and very secret. I don't think that I can quit. They always say that 'it won't go well for me' if I do."

"Are you sure that they aren't just being mysterious and cryptic without any muscle behind their threats?"

"No, I've seen them play. They are intense, and I think that they wouldn't stop at anything to teach a errant member a lesson. Speaking of that, was Billy ever in one of these clubs?"

Laughing, Colin replied, "I don't think so, I've taught him everything that he knows, and he tells me everything about his life, so I'm sure that I would have heard about it before now. Why do you ask?"

"One of these guys keeps talking about a Billy from Pittsburgh and it's making me nervous."

"That's very interesting Daniel, you know why the four of us are here. There was a S/M murder in Pittsburgh that Billy, and consequently, the rest of us were caught up in. Perhaps there's a connection here. If there is, you better talk to the police."

"They would kill me if I do. They are very particular about keeping the whole thing secret. The police are the last people I should talk to at this point."

"I'm not so sure that I agree with you, but there might be another avenue to pursue. I have a cousin who can usually find out anything or get anything done. Maybe, with your permission, I'll ask him to snoop around. He's involved in the leather community as well."

"Thanks, but there's another problem."

"Yes?"

"I've been more or less ordered to attend their next dungeon party sometime this month. If I tell Billy, I'm sure that it will create all sorts of problems right now, and I'm sure that he wouldn't be able to keep quiet about it."

"And if you don't go?"

"It won't go well for me..."

"Oh Daniel, how do we gay boys get involved in these things? At first glance, I would assume that they are being that weird kind of mysterious that is so rampant in the leather community. However, if you think that I'm wrong, I guess that you'll have to go. That is, if you feel that it's safe for you to go. Be evasive with Billy, I'll make sure that he's OK with it. It's going to be touchy right now, with the two of you moving in together and all, but I think that he can be made to understand. Just don't let him know right now that you are going to an orgy."

"You want me to lie to him?"

"Well, ordinarily I would never suggest that. Just be evasive and I'll tell him that it's a top's prerogative to be a little mysterious. Don't worry."

"I'm not sure how this leather thing works with someone you love, Colin. Are there rules and protocol that you follow? How do you conduct a life with someone when the basis of it is this dominance/submission thing?"

"Well Daniel, that's a good question. And it's a question that I have often wondered about, especially since meeting Derek. I'm not sure; I'm still in the process of working it out."

"Is this your first lover/leather relationship?"

"One of any substance, yes."

"Does it work?"

"Sometimes it does, and sometimes it doesn't. Every day is an adventure. If you express yourself as a top too strongly, you can be accused of being a tyrant, and if you are understanding and patient, you are accused of being a bad top. In many ways, the top is always walking a tight rope in these things."

"Why do we get involved in leather?"

"Each of us has our own reasons. Mine were personal."

"What were they, may I ask?"

"I was young. I had fallen in love with a beautiful man, a ballet dancer. He broke my heart. I didn't feel like getting involved with another man and really wanted to deal with all of the anger that I was experiencing. I walked into a leather bar and found an outlet. Interestingly enough, my cousin, Dominic, was doing the same thing at the same time. I found that I could really get intense with a guy. And I could do it repeatedly, and not have the emotional involvement that comes with a more conventional kind of coupling. Over time, I finally got tired of the whole thing and eventually settled down with a bad man as a lover. That lasted a long time, until I met Derek. Then we got together and I have been trying to integrate the whole thing ever since.

"Wow, that's the stuff of novels, Colin. Do you ever see the ballet dancer, your cousin, or the bad man lover any more?"

"Unfortunately the bad man lover lives in Columbus and we run into him on occasion. He's become an alcoholic and really is a mess now. My cousin is the man I talked about earlier, and let's not get involved anymore in his occupation or hobbies. The ballet dancer is dead now."

"AIDS?"

"The immediate cause of death was suicide. However, he might have been HIV positive, I don't really know. It was several years after our dalliance."

"I'm so sorry."

"Me too. You go through all of the things that people go through when someone they know and love commits suicide. Eventually I came to look at it as just another aspect of his life. He was a very passionate man. Suicide is ultimately a passionate way to die. So, he died as he lived."

"Ever think of writing your memoirs, Colin?"

"Not on your life. Parts would be so boring that people wouldn't read them, and parts would be so titillating that they wouldn't believe them. My life is best left steeped in mystery."

Daniel got up out of the chair and walked over to the counter where Colin was standing. He put down his glass, put his arms around Colin, and kissed him passionately on the mouth. The kiss lasted a lot longer than just a usual good night kiss between friends who had just shared a tender moment. As Daniel's hand slid down to Colin's crouch, Colin stopped him.

"Colin, will we ever get to have sex one-on-one?"

"You're amazing Daniel. You're conflicted about going to a dungeon party and having sex with a bunch of anonymous men, but you have no problems having sex with me, right here, two floors below where your lover is sleeping and waiting for you?"

Daniel just looked sheepishly at Colin. After a lingering moment, Colin lightly kissed him on the mouth, put his arm around him, and led him to the staircase. "In due time, Daniel, you and I will play again in due time."

They walked up the stairs together, with Colin opening the door to his bedroom where Derek and Al were sleeping, and Daniel continuing up to the third floor where his new boyfriend was sound asleep. Even young boys have to deal with having had just a little too much to drink and a little too much to eat at times.

Colin had a little trouble getting to sleep that night. Daniel had disturbed him. Not only the invitation to sex, but also the mysterious secret leather organization and the connection with Billy. He was sure that it had something to do with Brandy and what was going on in Pittsburgh and really wanted to get the police involved. He didn't want to put his friend in harm's way though. Of course, it could just be two gay men being a little over dramatic. Perhaps, Dominic was the best solution for this problem. He trusted Dominic, and always would. He didn't approve of what Dominic did for a living so he never confronted him on it, but he trusted that Dominic would always look after his interests and keep him, and now his leather family, safe. What to do about Daniel and his untimely interest in sex with him, he was clueless about. Now he felt a little guilty about suggesting that Daniel lie to Billy about the dungeon party. Why don't straight people have these problems? He tossed and turned while his two lovers slept.

Chapter 12

Billy was mad. They had only been living together a couple of weeks, and now Daniel was off somewhere for a weekend of something, and he wouldn't quite tell Billy what it was all about. Even though he was young, Billy knew that when men were evasive, they were usually lying. He also knew that when they lied, they usually cared more about the person that they were lying to than the person they were off doing heaven knows what with. Well, if Daniel has a secret lover somewhere, he could go out and get a trick. Or even better yet, get Colin to have sex with him. That would show Daniel. Daniel is always talking about how hot Colin is, it would only serve him right to miss out on having sex with Colin.

Colin was in the library on the phone when Billy walked in. He did what all cute, young, hot boys do when their sexual object is on the phone. He wondered about looking at the spines of books while seductively glancing at Colin from time to time.

"Billy, I hate to be rude, but this is a really private conversation. I'll come upstairs when I'm done."

Billy looked at Colin as if he had just lost his last friend. First Daniel and now Colin is treating him shabbily. He turned and walked out of the room and up to his floor and plopped himself down on the couch in his living room area, doing his best to make sure that Colin knew that we was pouting when he arrived.

Colin and Dominic finished their conversation rather quickly. It turned out that Dominic thought that he knew about this organization and knew someone who would give him the complete low down on what was going on, and why they were interested in Billy. After Colin hung up the phone he went upstairs to see what the boy wanted.

"Sorry about that Billy, it was very private."

"Everything around here seems private anymore. What's up with this? Daniel goes away for some lame excuse weekend and you don't want me to hear you on the phone."

"Billy, I know where Daniel is. Don't worry about it right now. All I can tell you is that he didn't want to go and there is no threat to your relationship in any way?"

"Are you lying to me like he did?"

"Of course not. Have I ever lied to you in any way?"

"Once you told me that it wouldn't hurt, and it hurt like hell!"

"OK, I deserved that one. But, really, I haven't lied to you. Perhaps misjudged a particular thing I was doing at the time, but I didn't lie."

"You're right, as usual. But tell me, what's going on with Daniel?"

"You'll know in time – let it go for right now. He loves you."

"He may love me but he wants a chance with you in the sack again."

"What makes you think that?"

"Are you getting ready to lie to me as well?" The younger boy asked, without the hint of a smile on his face.

"Of course not. I know, he's attracted to me, but he loves you."

"I'm attracted to you, and we're right here – fuck me."

"In a heartbeat boy, but will you be able to live with yourself after that? Remember, Daniel will come back, you will eventually find out what's going on, then you will feel a terrible sense of guilt, and you will have driven a stake between Daniel and me."

"Not a bad thing, right now."

"Come on Billy, being bitchy and jaded doesn't become you. You're far too young for that!"

"But I'm pretty, so I can be as bitchy and as jaded as I want."

"How about you and me going out to dinner. Derek and Al are busy somewhere, and we could have a nice quiet dinner and talk about old times."

"OK, but if I can't be bitchy, you have to pay. You *are* older, after all."

Colin and Billy got dressed and went out into the world. As they were comfortably sitting down to a nice dinner with a fireplace in the background, and hot waiters flirting with them, Daniel was stowing his gear in a rather poorly heated cabin, again, in the middle of nowhere in particular. The same cast of characters was here, and the same types of activities were going on. He wasn't in the mood for it, but he was going to make the best of it and pretend. Ben had already greeted him rather warily Daniel thought, and had given him the third degree once again, about a boy named Billy from Pittsburgh.

That night, Daniel got into an intense scene with two slave boys. There was an audience, and Daniel performed well for them. After it was over, Ben and a couple of other guys came over and literally congratulated him on how well it went. That was all that it took to win these guys over—

it seems that the reluctance that caused so much consternation on the phone had given way to acceptance by the upper echelon of the club. If they only knew that he was counting the minutes until it could be done and he could be back in bed with the very boy that they all seemed so concerned about.

The next morning, a special treat greeted the men. Not only did it snow the night before, but also they were bending their rules and were admitting a new member, out of the normal time sequence of receiving members only once a year. The man wasn't even here the night before, at least Daniel didn't think that he was there. He appeared in front of them in full leather, and did not kneel or experience any of the other things that Daniel had to experience. He was hot --- coal black hair and deep blue eyes that reminded him of Colin's eyes. He was a little on the short side, but with a body to die for, and perhaps the most handsome man that Daniel had ever scene. Obviously, there was something different about this man. He was given many special treatments. He turned and greeted a few of the other men. He eventually made his way to Daniel and simply held out his hand and said, "Hello, my name is Dom."

"I'm Daniel; boy did you get the special treatment today. No kneeling, piss, or flogging for you."

"I actually went through all of that years ago, in Germany. That was back in the days when everyone who wanted to be involved in this sort of thing had to do that."

"I have a friend in Columbus who had the same experience. And I thought that he was padding the story, so to speak."

"Columbus is a nice town."

"Where are you from?"

"Chicago actually."

"Do you have a lover back in Chicago?"

"Yes, I do. You wouldn't be hitting on me would you?"

"Well, maybe a little, but I have a lover as well. It's a relatively young relationship, and I hate being here."

"My lover and I have been together for a long time. Once we got over all of the cultural differences that we had, it's been rather easy. He wouldn't be threatened by this at all – a little irritated, but not threatened."

"What sort of cultural differences?"

"Well, I'm Italian and Catholic, and he's a Syrian Muslim."

"That's some cultural divide! I bet it was hard."

"The first five years with any man is hard – after that, it becomes easy. Trust me, no matter how saintly a person is, no matter how hot, how well balanced, no matter what. When two guys settle down, each of them assumes some characteristics of the Antichrist."

"Gee thanks, I guess I have a rough time ahead of it."

"Not really, it passes quickly, and doesn't seem as bad once it's over."

"Great. I take it that you have been to Columbus?"

"Yes, actually I come there quite a bit any more," Dom replied.

"You'll have to look me up when you're in town. I'll give you my number."

"I'm sure that our paths will cross. I don't really need your number."

After a few more pleasantries, they said goodbye. Daniel thought that Dom was a little abrupt, not asking for his number or anything. He seemed like one of the few nice people in this organization; but who knew, he might be just as crazy as the others. As he continued to endure his first weekend away from his lover and yet another weekend with these guys, Daniel seemed to start to get along with everyone. This surprised him. He thought for sure that he would be miserable the whole time. That made him feel guilty.

Meanwhile, back at home, the entire family was attending the liturgy at St. Peter's. Billy always felt a little out of place here, but was comfortable enough between Colin and Al. Derek's sermon was not one of his better attempts, but it seemed to past muster with the dwindling congregation. During coffee hour, Colin noticed that Derek looked withdrawn and distant from the people talking to him. He nudged Al, who agreed with Colin's assessment. When it was finally over, the three of them walked Derek back to the house.

When they were alone, Colin asked his lover of many years, "What's wrong?"

"It's just not there any more Colin. I don't know how much longer I can keep this up. I don't pray very much outside of the liturgy, and I think that it's beginning to show."

"At the risk of being too painfully honest, yes it is. But remember, sometimes we go through a period like this, spiritually. Maybe you should talk to Al about it."

"You have the same training as Al, and I trust you. Oh, don't get worried, I'm not going to chuck it all in right away. But the danger signs are there."

"Is everything all right with us?" Colin asked timidly.

"I think so."

"If you decide not to be a priest anymore, do you still want to live here?"

"It would be easier Colin, but I'm not sure what I would do for a living."

"Teach young boys at the little Episcopal school down the road."

"Oh yeah, that's right. Do I have to remind you that I am gay, HIV positive, and associated with a rather sordid murder back in Pittsburgh?"

"So, you'll be a teacher with a lot of character. The stuff of school legends and whatnot."

"You still OK with Al with us?"

"Of course, I like him. I know that he's a little tedious right now, but he's going through that Roman Catholic guilt thing about betraying God and all. He is a comfort to me in my struggle, I confide in him a lot."

"Good. So how do I get you out of this mood?"

"Colin, let me cook dinner tonight for all of us, then take me out for desert."

"Can I help cook?"

"NO! I want to be alone. Trust me, it will help. You go and diddle with Al or fuck Billy or something. When is Daniel coming back, and where was he exactly?"

"His flight arrives this afternoon, and I have to pick him up at the airport. It's funny, no one in Columbus ever drives themselves to the airport. They insist that people drop them off and pick them up. I just don't understand it."

"Perhaps because it was a small town for so long, but you haven't successfully dodged my second question, where was Daniel?"

"I can't tell you right now. I'm sworn to secrecy."

"May I remind you that we don't keep secrets from one another? Wasn't that your first rule?"

"Give me a little leeway on this one, Derek, please?"

"Is something wrong?"

"Perhaps, but I'm not sure. It's too soon to tell, and please don't hound Daniel when he comes home, I'm sure that Billy will be doing enough of that."

"Let's get this straight, Colin. I don't know where he is, and you can't tell me. His own lover doesn't know where he is and you aren't telling him. And, may I remind you, that you have spent significant time with your cock up his lover's ass, and still you won't tell him where Daniel has been?"

"Would you lay off, Derek? Go to the kitchen and start cooking."

"Umm.....that's as forceful as you have been lately. I like it. Any chance of continuing that downstairs later tonight?"

"A very good chance, boy. If you behave yourself."

As Derek went into the kitchen to start dinner, Colin went upstairs to read for a while. Eventually Billy came bounding down the steps to ask if he could go with Colin to pick up Daniel at the airport. While he didn't understand why Colin asked him not to go, he let the older man have his way. He took Colin's suggestion to go upstairs and make himself very pretty. Billy loved making himself pretty, and did so whenever he had the chance. He also spent a great deal of time checking himself to see if he remained pretty. Dinner and desert tonight would definitely be followed by a wonderfully romantic evening upstairs.

Colin arrived at the airport just as Daniel was coming out of the door. Coordination of effort never worked so well. When he got into the car, Daniel's first question was, "How is Billy, is he mad at me?"

"He might be a little irritated, and a lot confused, but I don't think that he's mad at you."

"Did he go out tricking while I was gone?"

Colin shook his head and gave a disgusted look at Daniel, "I'm not going to get involved in this whole thing. That's not fair, and I'm not going to answer the question, but no, he did not. At least, not to my knowledge."

"Sorry, I just don't want to screw this one up. And if you fucked him, I don't mind."

"Would you please stop this? How was your weekend, Daniel?"

"It wasn't too bad. They still give me the creeps, but I think that they trust me a little more now. A couple of them are really nice, but there aren't many of those. The rest of them are downright scary. Did you fuck Billy?"

"Would you please stop this? I'm not going to answer any of your questions. Did *those guys* have any more questions about Billy?"

"Always. He fascinates them. That's what is really scary."

"I have someone that I might want you to talk to. He's my cousin, actually. He might be able to help us in this."

"Cool. Is he in Pittsburgh, or Columbus?"

"He lives in Chicago."

"Wow, what a coincidence. I met the most gorgeous man from Chicago at this thing. You wouldn't believe how good looking and hot he is. Man, I could play with him anytime."

"What was his name?"

"Dom."

Daniel couldn't see the smile creeping across Colin's face. By that time they were pulling into the driveway with Derek, Al, Billy and Finocchio all waiting for Daniel. He couldn't believe that everyone was so happy to see him after only a couple of days away. Billy didn't even bring up the trip, or what it entailed, even once that night. The little family enjoyed a wonderful meal that Derek had prepared. After that, they went for desert. When they finally got back home, Colin, Derek, and Al went downstairs for what was to be the sexual experience of their lives. Billy and Daniel went upstairs, and while it was a more tender encounter, the effects were the same. Once again, everyone went to bed totally fulfilled that night. Everyone, that is, except Finocchio, who had to rely on treats from the cupboard as his many masters passed by his sentry position between the basement and the upstairs. It was funny how the dog always seemed to be guarding the kitchen.

Chapter 13

Dominic and his lover, Amin, arrived at the Columbus airport a few weeks later. Amin had never met Colin, and Dominic had never met Derek. Colin and Dominic managed to keep their separate lives and still maintain some semblance of communication. They were once lovers. That relationship was intense and they were young, but it wasn't completely monogamous. When they finally decided to part, Dominic did the unthinkable. Colin, and his first lover, David, were in the process of getting back together. Dominic slept with David. It almost destroyed both Colin and David. Dominic knew that he had crossed a boundary with Colin, however it was his ties to Italian organized crime led to the final rift between the two cousins. They still maintained a friendly but cordial relationship; a cordiality that lent a certain amount of coldness to their encounters. The simple truth was that they still both loved each other, and each would lay down his life for the other.

Dominic and Amin checked into one of the downtown hotels and rested a while before Dominic called his cousin.

"Hello," answered Colin.

"Hey, its me," Dominic replied, "What's up for tonight?"

"Well, perhaps the easiest way for us to do this is to meet at one of the leather bars and get the introductions all done there, on relatively neutral territory," Colin answered.

"Can we have a little time together, first?"

"Of course, Dominic, why don't we do dinner first, alone?"

"Great, I'll make reservations and call you later with the particulars," Dominic replied, and hung up the phone.

So the plans were made. They were all going to meet in one of the leather bars later that night. That way, the meeting would be informal, and, while contrived, at least a little more comfortable. Colin managed to get all of the players to agree to go out that night—no small feat, considering the fragile personalities of five gay men living together.

It was good that Colin and Dominic did manage to have a little time alone though. It would give them time to reconnect. Everybody else didn't seem to mind. Derek and Al were running late, and Daniel and Billy were doing whatever they did for dinner on Friday nights. Amin agreed to order room service, giving his lover and Colin a chance to catch up with each other.

Colin arrived at the rather fussy restaurant in the Short North and was immediately taken to his cousin's table. For as much history as the two of them shared, and a not always happy history at that, they were quite at ease with one another.

"Buona sera," Dominic said as he stood and embraced his cousin, kissing him lightly on both cheeks.

"Buona sera, caro mio," Colin replied.

"How have you been?"

"Well, other than somehow being drawn into a murder in Pittsburgh, getting a new job, moving to another city, acquiring a new boy, and having a couple move into the third floor, its been rather quiet. Any you?"

"Its nice to see that your razor sharp sarcasm still works," Dominic answered, laughing and lifting a wine glass to his lips. "My life is dull, except for Amin. You are going to love him. This might be the real thing for me."

They discussed the issue at hand for a while, Dominic outlining his take on the situation and what could be done about it. They then switched to the personal discussions that only former lovers or long time friends could have with one another.

"So, how are you and your little family doing these days?" Dominic asked while holding his wineglass up in the most seductive manner.

"Fine. Great actually. I can't believe that I'm living in a house with four other men, two of whom I have sex with regularly."

"Does that mean that you have sex with the other two irregularly?"

"Well, I have in the past. But for right now, I'm sticking with the two that I have."

"Monogamous, after a fashion?"

"Well Dominic, we still play around together and others are invited into our play, but a kind of monogamy."

"You know that Amin has always wanted to sleep with you."

"You know that Derek has always wanted to meet you."

Before the men could register their innermost fears that each would woo the other's lover away from him, they started to laugh.

"I miss you Colin."

"And I, you."

"I wish that we could live a little closer to one another. Perhaps we could settle our little differences and get on with being friends, not to mention, relatives."

"Well, move to Columbus."

"Amin would absolutely leave me, if not kill me first, then leave me. He hates Ohio, for some unknown reason. He feels more comfortable in Chicago. I guess it has to do with being Arabic and the sentiment against Iran and Iraq so strong, especially in, shall we say, less cosmopolitan places."

"Well, I can't just move to Chicago without some visible means of support."

"I could arrange some for all of you. You know that."

"Dominic, that's the last thing that I need right now. Besides, Derek has issues with *your* visible means of support."

"I hope that you mean my invisible means of support dear cousin. We don't want me too far out there in the spotlight, do we?"

"Whatever. But he really does have some moral issues with what you do."

"Just like you did? This must be a marriage made in heaven; you both think alike."

"Well, on some level, we do. But on other levels we most certainly disagree. Anyway, let's just try to get through tonight, and, hopefully, the rest of the weekend without you and me fighting -- and without you causing a fight between Derek and me."

"You must think that I'm a horrible person, that I can't handle myself in a touchy social situation."

"Oh no, dear cousin, I know your charm. I'm sure that you can. But let's just be on our best behavior."

The two men openly embraced and kissed before leaving one another on the street. What they couldn't have noticed, even if they were looking, was the table at the window of another restaurant with two rough looking men staring out at them. As Colin and Dominic walked away from each other, Ben turned to the other man and said, "Now, isn't that interesting. The man who our little Billy is living with knows our most recent member."

"I have a feeling that he knows the other Columbus member as well. I can only assume that if we wish to see the 'family' together, we should try to go to the local leather bar tonight."

"You're probably right, but I hate those places. They're for amateurs."

"Well, we will have to make sure that we are inconspicuous tonight – I brought full leathers and a cap – I even have some mirrored sunglasses. We can look like two old tops from the sixties. No one will recognize us."

As the two men continued to plot their surveillance of the boy they so wanted to punish, Colin made his way home and found the house full of activity. He wasn't sure why everyone was so excited about going out tonight, but boys and a puppy were running up and down the stairs between the floors, lending leather articles to each other and trying things on. He had to laugh.

"What's all the excitement about?"

"It's the first time that we have all gone out together, in leather, as the members of this household," a rather officious Billy told Colin.

"Billy, it's not a prom."

Al stuck his head out and sang, "Maybe we all need a little Christmas…."

"Or maybe just a little prom," Billy added.

"Or maybe none of us have been getting laid enough around here. You guys are really getting nuts," Colin said as he plopped down on his bed.

"I always get laid enough, Sir," Billy said as he saddled up to Colin on the bed.

"Don't we all know that!" Derek added, and the started to hit Billy with the pillow.

It didn't take long for them all to get ready. But it was far too early to go to the usual place, so they went to the most vanilla of the leather bars and had some drinks first. Colin knew that the group was too excited to go to the other bar without unwinding a little first. He also took the step of getting cabs for them tonight. He did that just in case they all had a little too much to drink—which is what he was planning for himself. The fact that Dominic and Derek would finally meet had him a little worried about how the evening would end up.

They walked into the other bar a little after midnight. It was filled with the usual cast of characters. Of course, as always, there was the strange council of older tops hidden in the shadows in the corner. That corner would be the place where blow jobs would be starting, as the time got closer to closing. Colin glanced over and saw the usual over weight guys, the Z-Z Top look-a likes, and a couple of well preserved older tops with their biker caps pulled way down low over their eyes with, of all things, mirrored sunglasses. Colin remembered when he tried that look earlier in his life, imitating the look of leather men from the seventies. He also remembered feeling foolish when he would walk into the unsuspecting pole because he couldn't see that well in a dark bar with sunglasses on.

Dominic and Amin were standing at the end of the bar, looking resplendent in very expensive and well-tailored leather. Derek grabbed

Colin and Al by their arms and said, "Man, look at those two hot guys."

Colin led his little group over to the bar. Daniel recognized Dominic right away, but was afraid to say anything, trying to maintain the requirement of secrecy that the leather club, the Knights of St. Germain, demanded of all who belonged.

"Dominic, I'd like to introduce my lovers, Derek and Al. This is Billy and Daniel—they live with us. Guys, this is my cousin, Dominic and his lover Amin."

Dominic started to shake hands and embrace the men. Al, Billy and Daniel did the same. Derek was a little taken aback at first, but soon joined in their camaraderie.

"Colin never told me that you were so good looking, Dominic," Derek said.

"I'm glad that we've finally had the chance to meet."

"I have to echo those sentiments. I have waited for some time to talk to you, Derek. Colin and I were once close."

"I know. I didn't realize that you were going to be in town now, did Colin know?"

"Actually, he did. In time, I'll explain it to you." Then Dominic quickly added, "Just excuse me a minute, I have to talk to Daniel. I met him recently."

As Dominic and Daniel started a quiet discussion away from the others, Colin and Amin spent some time talking to Derek, Al and Billy.

Dominic put his hand on Daniel's shoulder and said, "Daniel, I just want you to know that I'm looking into the situation with the Dark Knights of St. Germain."

"Oh Dominic, I'm so glad. I thought that you were a part of them and I didn't know who to trust in that organization." Daniel was, at the same time, both relieved and bewildered by the presence of Dominic and his association with Colin.

"Colin asked me to check into it. I had some connections and favors owed. I called them in. I can't tell you much right now, but I'll let you and Colin know more when I discover what its all about."

"Thanks," was all that Daniel could say.

"Let's go back and join the others. They will be wondering what's going on with us," Dominic concluded as he led Daniel back to the group.

The seven men were soon laughing and talking while they discussed everything except the murder in Pittsburgh or the leather group that Daniel had joined. They decided to excuse themselves from the bar and continue their festivities at the house. A succession of cabs was called to take them all back home.

While sex was definitely on the minds of all of the men, the energy just wasn't there—once home, they all changed into more comfortable clothes, Dominic and Amin borrowing some of Colin and Derek's sweats. They gathered in the second floor living room, in comfortable chairs with drinks and snacks that were hastily put together by Daniel and Billy. Colin and Dominic talked of old times, each retelling to the other how they met their respective lovers and what had happened over the years. Amin and Derek gently teased their lovers, recounting humorous moments from their time together. Al very comfortably sat at Colin's feet, listening with rapt attention as everyone talked about the history that they had shared with each other. Billy and Daniel were curled up together in one of the large chairs. It was the picture of domestic tranquility, everyone comfortable with each other, laughing and talking.

Meanwhile, back at the bar, the two men from the leather club, conferred with each other in whispers.

"Well, I guess we know why Daniel was so reluctant to come to our parties any more," Ben said to his older counterpart.

"Amazing that he and that boy from Pittsburgh managed to get together."

"What do you think about Dominic and this group? Why are they so close?" Ben asked.

"Well, I'm not sure about that one. Dominic and Colin seem to know each other very well. It might just be a coincidence. I don't think that Daniel was involved with any of these people before his initiation. And I am sure that he first met Dominic at the last gathering."

"I guess we'll have to decide what we want to do to that boy."

"Yeah, but tonight we should probably pick a nice boy to do something with to keep us in shape."

As they spoke, a rather skinny kid in bad fitting leather started staring at them. He was definitely interested, and probably a little inexperienced. It didn't take too long for the two men to notice him. Before long they had bought him a drink and he was kneeling in front of one of them, licking his crotch through the fabric of his leather jeans. By this time, the two older men knew that they had found some entertainment for the evening.

In another part of town, the seven men whose lives were so closely intertwined were having one of those conversations that go far into the early morning hours. Before they knew it, they realized that they had better go to bed if they didn't want to greet the sunrise without any sleep. Dominic and Amin decided to stay there and go check out of their hotel later. They would spend the rest of their time in Columbus, here, with the family. They were taken to the guest room at the other end of the hall from

Colin, Derek, and Al's room. As Colin climbed into his bed with his lovers, he said, "Man, this feels really good. I love it when we have the house full of hot men—especially hot men who make me feel so comfortable."

"I'm surprised that your cousin is so charming, I must have really misjudged him," Derek added.

Down the hall, Dominic and Amin were having a very similar conversation. Before long, all the men, and the small puppy were sound asleep in the comfort and safety of their home and family.

Much later, on a lonely road outside of the city, a young man staggered down a desolate highway. He had been thrown from a car after an evening of terror at the hands of two older leather tops. While they had not caused any permanent damage to the boy, the evening was anything but safe, sane or consensual. He wasn't even sure where they had taken him, but he was glad to be alive, if a bit bruised and shaken. They had been brutal. When he was tied to a cross he begged them to let him go. He offered to perform any sexual act with them, but they would not relent. They wanted to torture him, and he wasn't sure that there was any sexual component to it. It would be a long time before he ever picked up strangers in a bar again. He knew that he wasn't far from the city, and that the walk wouldn't take that long, but he was so weary; he was so frightened, and he felt so invaded.

It was about dawn when the man made his way into the center of town and managed to find a cab for the rest of the ride home. When he got there, he took off his clothes and took a long, hot shower. He moved as if in a trance. He was terribly thirsty, probably from having too much to drink the night before, and because he was often shouting out in pain during the leather tops' 'play'. He was happy to be home. He took some sleeping pills that were left over from a previous prescription from his doctor and nestled under the covers of his bed.

As the young man was fitfully drifting off to sleep, Colin and Dominic were up. They were walking Finocchio. The two cousins kept talking as if the years and their egos hadn't separated them at all. As they walked the dog, Derek and Amin sat at the kitchen table discussing their experiences with their respective lovers. Al woke up alone, and, shortly after waking, was greeted by the overwhelming feeling of sadness that he had come to know since leaving the priesthood. He was hoping above all hope that it would go away. Only Billy and Daniel slept in late that morning. Even Ben and his friend were up early that morning, discussing their plans for the boy who they felt had compromised their precious leather club's identity in the shadows.

Chapter 14

A couple of weeks later, Billy was at his mindless job in the bookstore in the Short North. It was a slow day. As he fiddled with the gay bumper sticker display, two older, rougher looking men entered the store. The two ignored all of the merchandise and just stared at Billy. He didn't take too much notice of them, he was just hoping for the day to end. He did, however, eventually take notice that they kept staring at him. But Billy, being Billy, just thought that they found him attractive. When they came to the counter with a couple of dirty magazines he felt obliged to do the sales clerk flirt with them.

"Well gentlemen, I see that you found what you were looking for," he said, smiling coyly.

"We certainly did young man. Has anyone ever told you how attractive you are?" The older of the two said.

"You are too kind to me, sir."

"That's the proper way of responding to me, boy," the older man replied, leering at Billy.

Billy, while knowing full well that they were talking of leather protocol, didn't quite feel comfortable in this place, with the way that he was dressed to involve himself in *that* kind of banter. Besides, they were definitely very unattractive, at least from his perspective. He rang them up and handed the two men their change.

"We could show you a very nice time some evening, boy. As a matter of fact, we could make it worth your while," Ben said as he accepted his change.

"That's OK, I'm with someone," Billy responded, trying his best to be friendly to, what he thought, was a typical customer.

"But you seem to be a boy that could use a little 'training', if you know what we mean," the older man added. "We are very proficient at showing you just how far you can go."

By now, Billy was feeling decidedly ill at ease with these two men. He was very happy when the manager-owner came from his office up to the cash register.

"Can I help out here? I'm David, I own the store," David said, addressing the two men.

"Oh no, not at all. We were just complimenting your help," Ben replied.

"From what I saw and heard on the in-store camera, I would say that you were bordering on harassing my help."

"Then please accept the apologies of two over-the-hill gentlemen. We hardly ever get the chance to talk to such an attractive, young man," the older of the two said. With that, Ben picked up the package and the two of them hurriedly walked out of the store.

"Thanks David, they were giving me the creeps," Billy said.

"That's OK Billy. Don't ever think that you have to take that kind of crap from anyone, just because he is a customer. If you don't invite, or graciously accept a customer's come-on, tell them so firmly."

The rest of the day passed in uneventful boredom for Billy. He almost forgot completely about the incident until he was at dinner that night in the house. They were all having dinner, with Dominic and Amin. Derek had spent the day cooking. Derek had been doing that a lot lately. It seemed that since he was toying with the idea of leaving active ministry in the Episcopal church, he spent a great deal more time around the house, doing domestic things.

The seven men were enjoying a truly wonderful meal. The conversation was going fast and furious and Billy didn't seem to have anything to add to it. He was desperately trying to think of something to say or to have some small opening in the conversation when he could add something. It finally came when Dominic said, "What are we going to do when we're old and can't attract men anymore?"

"Well, you *do* have me!" Amin said. "What am I, chopped liver?"

As the men were laughing, Billy finally felt that he had his chance to join the conversation. "Speaking of that, today two very unattractive men came on to me in the store."

"I'm sure that you have had your share of men, attractive and not so attractive, coming on to you in the store, Billy," Colin replied.

"This was very different. First, they were way older. Then, they were doing the leather top thing of telling me that I needed training, and that they could show me a lot of things, and all of that."

"So, what did you do?" Daniel asked.

"It turns out that David was watching on the camera. He came out and politely told them to leave, without using those exact words."

"And?" Daniel asked.

"That's the amazing thing. They just apologized and ran out of the store. I never saw anyone make such a complete reverse in my life!"

As the conversation continued, Colin gave a knowing look toward Dominic. Although it lasted for only a few seconds, paragraphs seemed to have been exchanged between the two men. Finally Colin broke back into the conversation, "Billy, does David keep those tapes of the store?"

"Yeah. I think that he keeps them for a month, then tapes back over them. Why?" Billy answered.

"Would he let me take a look at them?"

"Colin, why on earth would you want to do something like that? You're not doing the cowboy thing on your high horse again, making some kind of leather top statement that your property is to be respected or anything, are you? May I remind you that Billy is Daniel's responsibility in that department. And besides, it seems like a kind of harmless thing to me!" Derek spit out, almost yelling at his lover.

The other six men around the table were stunned to silence. No one expected such a caustic commentary on the situation from Derek, of all people. Al and Daniel just looked at each other, while Billy sat staring at Derek. Colin was terribly hurt by the off-the-cuff remark from Derek, but he was trying his best not to show it. Finally, it was Dominic who decided to bring the situation down a notch or two on the Richter scale.

"Derek, you might not realize this, and I can understand why, but Colin may have a very good reason to look at the tapes. You see, Daniel has joined some mysterious leather club. While there, he met a man who was very interested in the murder in Pittsburgh, and in Billy. It seems that this man feels that Billy somehow managed to cause a leak in the organization's wall of secrecy. They have been asking Daniel about Billy the whole time. These two men today could have been from that organization."

"Oh Dominic, I'm sorry. I didn't know," Derek replied.

"You don't have to be sorry to me. You didn't yell at me," Dominic answered.

As Derek turned to his lover, Colin said, "That's OK," even before Derek could form the words of an apology.

"Do you belong to this organization as well?" Derek asked Colin.

"No, I don't"

"Don't you think that Daniel should view the tapes then?" Derek continued, trying to regain some credibility in his lover's eyes.

"Actually, I was going to ask Daniel and Dominic to look at them with me."

"Dominic, are you part of this group?" Derek asked.

"I just recently joined when Colin asked me to look into this."

Billy, who had been stunned by Derek's outburst, finally regained his composure. "You guys mean that you have known about this for a while and haven't informed me of it? Don't you think that I have the right to know when someone could potentially harm me? Why didn't you tell me?"

Billy was looking right at Daniel, who seemed to be at a loss for words. The answer finally came from Colin. "Billy, we couldn't tell you right away. I found out about it when Daniel went to their last meeting. We didn't want to concern you until we were sure."

"Don't you think that I have the right to make those decisions. After all, it was me that Brandy tried to kill, and it's me that these guys probably want to kill right now."

"Before we get too hyper about this whole thing, let's just try to determine if the activity in the store today has to do with this leather club or if it was just two unattractive horny old men trying to pick up a little afternoon delight," Dominic added.

"And once you determine that? What happens then?" Billy continued.

"I'll tell you what should happen. You should go to the police. I'm not very comfortable with Colin and Dominic trying to stop this using only their own resources. We *do* have laws in this country to protect people." Derek answered.

"Don't worry, Derek. We plan on taking the information to the police. Dominic was just here to help find out that information. We aren't going to do this on our own," Colin replied.

Needless to say, it was a quiet evening in the household that night. Billy was still a little miffed about Daniel's involvement in this thing without letting him know. Derek was a little put off by Colin calling on Dominic to get involved without telling him. Al felt completely left out by the whole thing and Amin was just trying to be the perfect Mafia wife, sitting around, looking pretty, and keeping his mouth shut. Derek and Billy went to bed early that night. Amin and Dominic took Al out for a drink, leaving Daniel and Colin alone downstairs. Neither one of them wanted to go to their respective rooms until their lovers had the chance to cool down a little. Colin did what he always did when Derek was a little angry with him; he went downstairs to the basement to do laundry; it wasn't too long before Daniel came looking for him.

"Hey, are you hiding?" He asked Colin.

"Trying to. Get used to it. When they are mad at us, it's best to leave them alone for a while. Most of the time, everything then gets back to normal."

"And for those times when it doesn't?"

"You have to rely on your own resources to come up with what will cause peace to 'break out' in your home."

"I have to thank you for everything, Colin; you really have been a true friend. I never thought that when we all went home together several months ago, that I would end up living here, and that I would have you as a confidant."

"If we don't stop being such confidants, we might end up having only each other. We can't continue making our lovers angry with us," Colin said while he folded T-shirts.

"Well, I could think of worse people to end up with." As Daniel finished what he was saying, he put his arm around Colin's neck and pulled him over and kissed him passionately on the mouth. While he was kissing him, Daniel's hands found Colin's crotch and started caressing it. It didn't take too long for Colin to have the hard-on that Daniel was trying to effect. It was a strange characteristic of Colin, and apparently one that was shared by Daniel; when their lovers were mad at them, sex was very much on their minds. It was almost an uncontrollable thing. For the first time since Daniel and Billy got together, Colin responded to Daniel's advances.

It didn't take too long for the two of them to be out of their clothes and going at it like teen-age boys. It was as if the two of them had not had sex in a long time. Part of it had to do with the forbidden nature of what they were doing. The unspoken agreement had been that it was too early in Daniel's relationship for him to have sex with Colin, without Billy being present. Somehow tonight, because their lovers had put down both of them, all bets were off.

They kissed passionately for a while, and then, Colin rolled Daniel over. He got up and went into the dungeon and got a condom. When he came back he fucked Daniel roughly. As he was pounding Daniel's ass, Colin whispered, "Don't you dare cum." It didn't take Colin too long before he was cumming—it seemed like he was cumming for several minutes. As soon as it was over, he pulled out and threw the condom on the floor. He turned Daniel over and devoured his cock with his mouth. In a few minutes, Daniel disobeyed the initial order not to cum. He expected Colin to pull away, but Colin remained there, his mouth on Daniel's cock, swallowing Daniel's cum. When it was finally over, Colin came back up to Daniel's mouth, and kissing him, spit some of Daniel's cum into his own mouth. Then the two of them lay there, on the floor in the basement with dirty laundry all around them. They stared into each other's eyes.

"I can't begin to tell you how incredible that was," Daniel finally said. "I'm sorry about cumming in your mouth."

"Don't be sorry, it was what I wanted."

"Colin, I am negative.

"I'm sure that you are."

"It's just that I don't usually cum in someone's mouth, given the age that we live in and all."

"And Daniel, I don't usually let someone cum in my mouth. And I haven't swallowed it for many years. Obviously with Derek's condition, I can't do that with him."

"It felt great."

"My sentiments exactly. But remember. This is between us. I have a reputation as a hard-ass top in this house."

"I know. I just wish I could pull off the top thing with the same force that you do."

"You will in time."

"Colin, this might just change everything. I can't even begin to tell you how wonderful that whole thing felt."

"I think that I felt it to. But remember, we're both feeling kind of slighted by our lovers. I'm sure that made it feel even better."

The two men, acting like they had just shared a piece of stolen cookie, cleaned themselves up and straightened up the laundry. They went back upstairs, each going into his own room, and each returning to his lover. When Colin slipped into bed with Derek and Al he felt at home. Strangely, it didn't make him regret what he had just done. It only made the warmth of his lovers' bodies even more comforting. Daniel didn't have it quite as easy. Billy wanted to know everything about the leather club and why Daniel didn't mention all of this before. When it was over, Billy seemed satisfied. He was ready to have sex with Daniel who was falling asleep as the sun was rising.

The next day, Daniel, Dominic, and Colin visited the bookstore and looked at the tapes with David. Daniel could name Ben, and he recognized the other man, but didn't know his name. The three men conferred quickly about what to do. It was decided that Colin and Billy would go to the police and inform them of what was going on. They would give the police Daniel's name so he could confirm the interest that the two men had in his lover.

Billy was less than thrilled to be riding to the police station with Colin. He had a gay man's fear of the police. Colin simply had a distrust of them in general when it came to gay issues. They arrived at the station after a ride in which neither man said more than five words.

Colin approached the desk sergeant and got his attention with a quiet cough. "Sir, I have a problem that might need some police involvement, and I'm not sure who I should speak to."

"What sort of problem would that be, sir?" The sergeant asked.

"I think that my friend here may be in danger. There seems to be a couple of guys who are out to do him harm."

"How do you know that?"

"It's kind of a long story, and I would gladly tell you, but I would rather only tell it once, and to the person I'm going to have to tell it to," Colin replied, standing his ground.

"You two go over there and sit down, I'll call one of the detectives."

Colin and Billy went to the chairs that were arranged on the side of the room furthest away from the desk and the desk sergeant. They waited for what seemed to be quite some time. It seems that the sergeant may have tolerated Colin's strong willed persistence, but he wasn't about to let it go without teaching him a lesson on some level or another. Finally, an attractive middle-aged detective appeared in the doorway and waved for Colin and Billy to follow him.

They were led down a narrow hallway and into a rather cramped room. The detective's desk had a picture of a pretty woman and two small children on it, with several pictures that had probably been drawn by one of those two children. So far, the detective had spoken not one word. Finally, once he sat down, he said, "Hello gentlemen, I'm Detective Marshall. How can I help you?"

Colin relayed the story of the murder in Pittsburgh and the attempted murder of Billy by Brandy. He told him of the testimony at the trial of a mysterious person who was involved in the 'training' of Brandy Mantune. Then he methodically told the detective of Daniel and the people that he met at the leather events that he had been attending, and finished by retelling Billy's story of the two men in the book store and showing the detective the tape. The story was told with Colin's unyielding scientific sense of telling the facts and the facts alone. When it was over, he sat quietly while the detective looked from Colin to Billy and then back to Colin again.

"Mr. Morgan, you and your friend here caused quite a stir in Pittsburgh, right?" The detective asked.

"I'm not sure if we caused quite a stir or not. We did somehow get involved in this whole sordid scandal, but we didn't do anything to cause our involvement."

"But you were involved. And you had to leave Pittsburgh because of it."

"We didn't *have* to leave detective, we *chose* to leave."

"Mr. Morgan, the bottom line is that you were involved and that, because of the scandal, you had to leave your home city and come here."

"Officer, may I say something?" Billy asked.

"Yes?" The detective inquired.

"We didn't want to come here—I mean to the police. But I don't want to go through what I went through in Pittsburgh. Can we get to the real issue here, I'm in danger."

"It sounds like you two invite danger by associating yourself with these perversions, and groups surrounding them," the detective said dryly, looking into Colin's steel blue eyes.

"Wait a minute, detective, that's not fair. What we do is our own business. Your business is to protect us," Colin replied with the same dry, almost monotone, voice that the detective had used.

"Mr. Morgan, I'm just saying that if you would stay away from these places and people, maybe you wouldn't be having these problems. And, while we're at it, have the two men that you are talking about made any specific threats against the young man here?"

"They were certainly creepy enough for me," Billy added without prompting.

"Detective Marshall, I agree with you. There haven't been specific threats, but the circumstances are pretty suggestive that they wish to do some harm to Billy. I was hoping to avoid that *before* it happened. I thought that if we gave you the tape, and you could identify the people involved, maybe we could prevent it!" Colin said vehemently, betraying the cool exterior he had heretofore displayed.

"Well, tell you what Mr. Morgan. I'll keep the tape. I'll watch it. If they did anything wrong, I'll investigate further. I assume that Billy's 'lover' will substantiate what you have already told me.

Colin realized that he was getting absolutely nowhere with the detective. He answered him in a coldly cordial manner and got up to leave. Billy, ever true to form, followed Colin's lead. The detective led them down the hall, out into the room that they first encountered when they entered the police station. They said their good-byes with the detective promising to do whatever he could, given the situation.

Once inside the car, Billy was furious. Mercifully for Colin the ride home was rather short. Al, Derek, Daniel, Amin, Dominic, and Finocchio, all waiting for a report about their trip to the police station, pensively greeted them.

"I can't believe they were so cavalier about the whole thing! This is my life we're talking about here," Billy exclaimed as the group gathered around the kitchen table to hear the news.

"Billy is right. They were of no help. As a matter of fact, they kind of indicated that this was our entire fault. Something about the type of people we hang out with. Although they didn't actually say the words, it was like, you lie down with dogs, you come up with fleas," Colin added.

"I could have told you that." Daniel joined in. "The Columbus police department is not particularly gay friendly. And they are a mean group of people."

"I'm not sure what our next step should be," Colin said, looking around the table.

"Well, I can be of some assistance, here. Protection is my game, you know," Dominic finally interjected.

"Under normal circumstances I wouldn't counsel for *that* type of help, but given the situation, and the fact that Billy might be in danger, I guess that's the only recourse that we have," Derek said with some finality.

"What kind of help are we talking about here? Or am I just supposed to sit back and let people decide my fate!" Billy said with increased tension in his voice.

"Billy, let's just say that I have the means to protect people," Dominic answered. "And I think that I can help here."

"And just exactly what do you do?" Billy asked.

"Billy, some things are better left unsaid," Colin answered.

"That's all right for you to say. These guys aren't after you! What am I supposed to do? This entire mysterious act is fine during a play scene, but right now I don't think I want to play this game. Can someone please be a little more forthcoming with some information? My life is at risk here."

"Billy, it might not just be your life… "Derek started to say, but was cut off by Billy,

"What do you care? You always wanted rid of me anyway!"

"Wait one minute! This is pathetic! We aren't going to start to fight among ourselves because the police won't help us! Billy, Derek loves you dearly, that was unfair, and would you please be patient and trust us a little to help you!" Colin said, standing up to make his point a little more emphatic.

No one said a word. Obviously, since Colin was standing, he had the floor, and the group seemed willing to listen to him. "First of all, we are aware of the danger. I'm sorry that the police aren't quite as aware of that as we are, but that's just the way it is. We all live in this house, there are five of us, so we can watch out for each other. We just have to be a little careful when we leave, and we should make sure that Billy is never alone. As for Dominic and what he does or does not do for a living, that is no one's concern here. He can help us. That's all that we need to know right now. He will help us if needed. And we should be grateful that he is willing to do this. Now, can we possibly get back to living a somewhat normal existence?"

"Will this saga never end?" A weary Derek asked.

"Yes, it will end. Perhaps not as quickly as you thought, but it will end," Dominic predicted with authority.

As the group contemplated the future, they seemed to grow quiet, almost calm. After a couple glasses of wine, they decided to go out for dinner that night. An unsettled peace descended over the group, almost a resignation to a fate not yet discovered. Eventually, they came back home and started to pick of the pieces of their lives. Colin just hoped that Dominic's prediction was right; that it would end, but that it might just take a little longer than they originally expected.

Chapter 15

Millicent's consecration as a bishop was soon approaching. In addition to the gnawing problems with Billy and the ominous leather man, Derek was having more and more difficulty fulfilling his responsibilities as a priest to his parish. While Colin was at work, with Billy and Daniel out of the house, he and Al finally had a chance to sit down and talk candidly about everything.

"Al, when did you finally know that you didn't want to be a priest any more?" Derek asked.

"Derek, I don't think we have traveled down the same path. Remember, I left to be a part of a relationship. My vocation forbade such a relationship. You have a different experience, for you, priesthood no longer offers the same challenges and rewards that you first expected from it. Are you sure that this isn't a burn-out issue going on?"

"I'm not sure Al. Has Colin ever talked to you about this?"

"No, why?"

"He has a theory about me. And, as much as I hate to say that he is right, I think that he might be. He says that I'm really good at beginnings, but that the long haul is what I have trouble with."

"Was he talking specifically about your priesthood, or was he talking about your relationship?"

"It was in the context of a discussion about us, early on. He's right; I can never stick with something for a long time. When it has come to men, in the past, I would try to end the relationship at the drop of a hat. Colin thinks that I try to push people away so that I am never the one who is abandoned, that I'm the one abandoning the other person."

"Do you do that, Derek?"

"I guess that I do sometimes. You see, I was always threatened as a child that my mother would leave me, unless I was good. Maybe threatened isn't the right word. I guess that when I did something bad, she appeared to be cold and distant. Once I grew up, I always had that fear, so I made sure that I was the one who left the relationship first. Needless to say, most of my relationships didn't last very long. And Colin was pretty astute to pick up on the fact that I would try to drive the guys away."

"You think that's what is going on with you and the priesthood?"

"Maybe a little, being a gay priest and all. But mostly it's a mind set. I have a real hard time getting really into sex, and then getting up and celebrating a liturgy. There are times when I'm in the middle of a prayer, and all of a sudden, I get a mental picture of something that I've done with Colin and you. It's pretty disconcerting. I'm not sure what it is that bothers me about it. And, this is really hard work. You know that. It can be emotionally draining. You and Colin are understanding when I come home completely empty, but both of you deserve better than that."

"And you think that we would leave you because of that?"

"I'm not sure."

"Well, I can honestly tell you this Derek. As complicated and multi-layered as Colin is, he's pretty easy to keep happy. He likes to role over, touch us, and know that we are in his bed. He likes us to show some submission occasionally during sex, and always in a bar. Those are pretty easy."

"He can be difficult at times, Al."

"Can't we all? Wasn't Billy calling you *la malcontenta* not to long ago?"

"Yes, but Billy and I have our own issues. And I feel guilty about those issues, especially with this dark force that seems to be following him. Anyway, we've really gone off the track. I'm going to try to remain a priest for a while longer, just because it's easier for everyone concerned."

"You know that we would support you – emotionally and financially, if we had to."

"Obviously you have never seen me when I didn't have anything to do. Ask Colin about it sometime."

"When is Millicent's ordination?"

"Two months hence. And I haven't a clue how I'm going to interact with her once she is my boss."

"Aren't you just completely in trauma on several levels."

"Not to mention that someone living in our home is being hunted down by mad gay SM terrorists, and there is a member of the mafia living with us. Just your typical average middle American family here; one ex-Catholic priest involved in a three way marriage, a boy slut, his crazy lover, our *pater familias* and his Italian thug cousin with a Syrian lover."

"What you're saying Derek is that we aren't exactly role models for the gay community's emphasis on acceptance?"

"You can say that again. Let's go somewhere and try to forget all of this."

Derek and Al decided a trip to the local Borders was in order. They could browse and get refreshments, and forget the world, for just a little bit. While they were driving there, Colin was finishing up his day at the hospital. He really felt like he had been in this same situation before. The problems at the Columbus hospital were very similar to the ones he was always dealing with in Pittsburgh. His mind was drifting. He was to meet Dominic at a bar right after work to discuss what they were going to do. They had to do something rather soon, Dominic and Amin had been in Columbus much longer than they had originally planned.

When Colin arrived at the bar, Dominic was holding court with a bevy of younger, very attractive men. Colin came over, pecked his cousin on the cheek, and whispered, "I'm going to tell Amin," before sitting down at the table.

The younger men, thinking that Colin was Dominic's lover soon drifted off to other parts of the bar. That was a good thing because Colin really wanted to discuss the situation with Dominic alone—and away from everyone in the house.

"Well, Dom, what are we going to do about this?" Colin asked.

"I could take care of it rather easily, Colin. The old fashioned way."

"I'm not sure that I'm comfortable with the direction that this is going. I don't approve of hurting or killing anyone. And, it would put you at too much risk. You can't always escape the law, you know."

"We could send them a message; make them stop."

"Dom, what about the other men that they would harm? These guys are really on the outer psychotic fringe of the SM world."

"Colin, it's not the first time. You and I have always heard the stories about crazy tops who go to far. It's just a part of our lifestyle."

"I always thought that most of that was urban legend."

"I'm sure that a lot of it is, but I'm also sure that there are crazy people out there who just don't know when to stop."

"So what you're saying dear cousin, is that we wait?" Colin said, looking around the bar.

"They are going to try to get Billy soon. We can show them that we mean business and scare them into stopping the craziness. The craziness in their lives, personal and corporate, as in the leather club."

"I'm not sure what to do. I just wish that the police would have been more helpful," Colin replied.

"Why would you think that they would be helpful? By and large, the police are not very happy with our lifestyle here."

As the conversation continued, both Dominic and Colin noticed the young attractive man, obviously interested in them. He kept staring at them. Both Dominic and Colin unconsciously returned his gaze. After a few minutes, the waiter appeared at their table with a fresh set of drinks for the two men, compliments of the young man at the bar. Taken aback for only a second, Colin raised his glass and toasted the young man, inviting him over to the table.

"Thank you for the drinks," Colin said as the young man sat down.

"You two are really hot," he said, and then added, "My name is Frank."

"Hello Frank, I'm Dominic, and this is Colin," Dominic answered smiling at the young man.

"I've never seen you guys in here. Are you from out of town?"

"Well, Dominic is from Chicago, but I live right here in Columbus," Colin answered.

"So, you two aren't lovers?" He asked.

"We were, a very long time ago," Dominic answered.

"Well, if the two of you are interested, I'm game for a nice three way tonight," the boy replied.

As Colin and Dominic were enjoying a pleasant exchange with the younger man, Al walked into the front of the bar. He and Derek had spent a pleasant afternoon in Borders, and then Al dropped him off at the house, saying that he had to return a book to the library. Colin was surprised to see Al entering the bar. Al, much to his disadvantage, couldn't see Colin or Dominic in the back of the bar. As Dominic continued a playful flirtation with the younger man, Colin watched as Al was greeted by another man and sat down to have a drink with him. Very soon, the other man was literally mauling Al, who didn't seem to mind it at all. After a few minutes, they left.

When Colin returned his attention to the men at his table, he realized that he had not been paying close attention to the conversation at hand. Dominic was more than willing to have a three way with the new man at the table, if only to have a chance to have sex with his cousin again. Colin put an end to the plans that the two men were making, saying that it was time that they both returned home to their lovers. Needless to say, the young man was completely disappointed. Colin, sensing his disappointment, gave him his number, saying that he should come over some time for dinner or drinks.

When Dominic and Colin returned home, Derek and Amin were busy preparing probably the best mid-eastern dinner that any of them had ever eaten. The four of them spent a great deal of time over dinner, drinking far too much wine for the middle of the week, especially since Dominic and

Colin had already had a few drinks in the bar on High Street in the Short North. Billy and Daniel were upstairs having a quiet family dinner with just the two of them. Al was still nowhere to be found.

After dinner, Dominic went out and rented a movie. He and Colin, along with Derek and Amin, curled up on the couch in the second floor living room and watched it. After the movie, Dominic and Amin retired to their room early, to have sex and fall asleep. Derek said that he had some paperwork to complete in his office, and Colin went downstairs to get Finocchio and take him for a walk.

As he was returning to the front of the house after the long walk, Al was parking his car in the driveway. "Late night, boy. Have you been working too hard at school?" Colin shouted out to alert Al to his presence.

"Oh…yeah. I've been really behind lately," a nervous Al said as he joined Colin and started to play with Finocchio.

"You should take it a little easier. You know what they say, too much work and no play. . ." Colin said as the two of them sat down on the steps of the front porch.

"I just have so much work to do, Colin," Al answered.

"I know. Well, don't drift off from us."

"You're right. I shouldn't. It's just been a little difficult lately. You know, the priesthood thing and everything else. And, it's hard being a student again."

"Al, remember, we're your family. We would like to be there for you when you need it."

"I know. And I know that I have been putting some distance between us lately. I just felt overwhelmed, and little left out some times."

"Why do you feel left out?" Colin asked.

"You and Derek have such a strong bond. It's amazing."

"We do. But that is from years of being together. We'll all be that way some day soon."

"How do you get there," Al asked, finally turning to face Colin.

"Honesty," was Colin's one word answer as he stared deeply into Al's eyes.

Al was clearly ill at ease. He felt bad enough having just had sex with another student from graduate school. He didn't need to have this conversation with Colin, and he was beginning to believe what Derek referred to as the special powers that leather tops have. He was silent as Colin took his hand.

"Al, you're at a disadvantage here. I was in the bar tonight with Dominic. I saw what happened."

Al was flabbergasted. He couldn't believe his bad luck. A thousand things were going through his mind. He didn't know what to do. He didn't even know why he had sex with that guy; it just felt so uncomplicated. He didn't know what to say to Colin, who was sitting there so patiently. After what seemed to be an eternity, Colin finally broke the silence, "Al, it's OK. Don't worry about it."

"Colin, I'm so sorry. It's not what you think. It just seemed so easy and so…"

"Uncomplicated!" Colin answered.

"How did you know?" Al asked.

"Give me a little credit Al. You just left the priesthood and fell in love with two men. You had to move to another city and then two other men moved into the same house with us. It's a little mixed up—even for gay standards."

"But I love you two and I don't want to mess it up," Al said as he started to cry.

Colin cradled Al in his arms and comforted him. "Don't worry Al. You didn't mess it up. Everything is going to be OK."

The two men sat there on the front porch steps as Finocchio struggled to get free from the tight hold that Colin had on his leash. After a while, they went back into the house. By now, the house was quiet, with everyone having already gone to bed. Colin led Al down to the basement. He ordered him to take off his clothes, and strapped him to the St. Andrew's cross in the dungeon. He then took his flogger off the wall and started to beat the man's back. Colin was relentless—increasing the intensity of the beating as the time went on. Al was writhing on the cross. When Colin felt that he had done enough, he let Al down – forcing the man to his knees and then pissing all over him. Colin then started to masturbate right in front of Al's face. After a few minutes, Colin came, spewing cum all over Al's face and hair. When he was done, he said, "Clean up down here boy, and come up to the kitchen."

As Colin was enjoying a glass of iced tea, Al finally came up to join his lover. Colin put his arm around Al and pulled him closer. They remained there, silent for the longest time. Al finally let out a huge sigh and relaxed in Colin's arms. Colin knew that he had achieved his goal. He looked deeply into Al's eyes and said, "Do you feel better now?"

"Yes Sir, I do."

"I'm glad. Now, let's try to get this relationship back on track. We all have given up too much to let it just dissolve from lack of attention."

"Yes Sir," Al answered.

"Al, let's not let Derek know about what you did earlier, it would just complicate his life even more."

"No Sir, I won't"

"Are you sure that you're OK?"

"Yes, I am. How did you know what I really needed tonight?"

"I love you – that's how I knew."

The two men walked arm in arm up the stairs, passing Finocchio who continued to fulfill his responsibility of guarding the kitchen against anyone who would dare try to steal the garden of earthly delights that was hidden within the confines of the refrigerator. Colin and Al joined Derek in bed, who merely moved over and groaned when the two of them curled up beside him.

Chapter 16

Billy couldn't believe that the people living in his house were guarding him. He felt like a prisoner, always having someone escorting him to or from work. Daniel was being really over possessive at the moment. In a way, he liked all of the attention. In another way, he really wanted a little freedom. Yes, he was a leather bottom, but he was also young and pretty, and he needed a little leeway here and there. This morning, Dominic drove him to work at the bookstore and tonight, Amin was supposed to pick him up late. Amin was really hot. Billy wondered if he could get him to fool around a little. Daniel had been so worried lately that he hardly touched Billy anymore – at least hardly touched him in the way that he wanted to be touched – rough and intense.

The bookstore was really boring today; no one came in to shop. After several hours, a few lesbians did start to browse, but they hardly bought anything. Billy couldn't believe that he had to be here until ten o'clock tonight. Daniel had told him that he really didn't have to work, but Billy thought that it was important that he kept his job.

As Billy occupied himself by counting the hours until the store would close, Colin was sitting through yet another boring meeting at the hospital. While his office *was* spacious, and contained windows, the geography of Columbus was so flat, that he could only see the campus out of it. There was nothing to distract him from the issues at hand. As Beverly, the crusty old nursing director, was groaning on about something or the other, Colin's mind drifted. He felt that his whole existence as a hospital administrator would end up with him listening to one minor official after another lament the state of health care at their particular institution. Beverly was from the old school—lots of hard work and a dedication to the institution. She had only worked here, at this hospital. In the twenty odd years of her career, she managed to climb the corporate ladder to the highest position available for a nurse. In many ways Colin admired her—and in other ways he felt very sorry for her. She was gifted, intelligent, and innovative. But the institution stilted her creativity, and since she was determined to stay here, she was trapped at this level of her career ladder. Any further advancement would be impossible. When the meeting finally ended, he was at a loss to remember anything from the last twenty minutes or so. Hopefully his secretary had kept accurate notes.

In another part of the campus, Al sat through one of the most fascinating lectures that he had ever attended. The only problem was that he couldn't keep his mind on what was being said. He kept going over the previous night's conversation with Colin. He hoped that he hadn't driven a wedge between them. He loved Colin and Derek and wanted to continue a life together with them. His exploration of relationships, leather, and a three-way marriage had just begun.

Meanwhile, Derek was dealt with his own demons. His lukewarm approach to his duties as a priest, along with the upcoming consecration of Millicent as his bishop had his mind preoccupied as well. He just couldn't get his thoughts organized around anything else, not even the predicament that Billy had found himself in at the moment. He was glad that he and Al had a long talk the other day. It helped. He knew that he was being distant from both Al and Colin, and he knew that Colin was hurt by it. Maybe after the festivities surrounding Millicent's assuming the position of bishop he could get back on track with his lovers, and with life in general.

That evening everyone in the house did dinner on their own, and each of the men occupied himself once at home. Dominic was visiting some old friends that were in Columbus. It was Amin who was supposed to go to the bookstore and pick Billy up at nine thirty that night. Amin had decided to have dinner out, alone. He had a really riveting novel and, after dinner, established himself at a window table in the coffee shop near the bookstore. Here he could drink strong black coffee and while the hour or two away waiting to escort his ward back to the safety of his house.

At nine thirty precisely, Amin walked the half a block up to the bookstore and greeted Billy as he was locking up the store. "Hey there, little one, how are you tonight?" Amin said as he placed he hand on Billy's shoulder.

"I'm doing OK – for a prisoner," Billy replied.

"It's only temporary Billy, and we're doing this because we care about you."

"I know that, but it still is irritating anyway. I can't go anywhere by myself. I haven't been to a bar or anything else, alone. I feel that I will never have a minute alone again."

"Well then, how about you and I go down the street and have a couple of drinks? It looks like you could use them," Amin said, taking Billy's hand in his as they walked south on High Street. Amin, despite his Islamic heritage, was definitely an out gay man. He had no qualms about walking down a busy city street holding another man's hand. He didn't even stop when a carload of college boys drove by them yelling "Faggot!" He just continued on with Billy until they reached the bar.

They were a striking couple—Billy with his blond hair and blue eyes, and Amin with his dark Syrian complexion. They caused more than a couple of heads to turn when they entered the bar. For once, the haughty waiter aggressively flirted with them. Flirted out of true desire and not just from trying to get a bigger tip. Amin was doing his best to try to pry Billy out of his depression. Neither one of them thought anything about it when another attractive man brought two drinks to the table complements of an admirer who wished to remain anonymous.

Amin just laughed, "Billy, who would want to buy us drinks and want to remain anonymous? Isn't the purpose of buying someone a drink so they will talk to you and you can pick them up?"

"I don't know Amin, but I don't question things in my life anymore. When you get into this much of a mess, you just go on autopilot," Billy responded. "Maybe after we're finished with these drinks our well-meaning suitor will reveal himself. Of course, what would the two of us do with him?"

Billy was just as confused. Actually, he was disappointed. He wanted to see what kind of man he was still capable of attracting, now that he was an old married person.

As they were enjoying their drinks, the man that they had assumed was a waiter disappeared into the crowd. No one took notice of the two older men giving him a twenty-dollar bill when his short errand was complete. Those around their table just thought that he was a paid companion for two older lovers looking for a little excitement for the evening. Ben was quite discreet when his stooge brought the drinks to the table first. Not even their unwitting accomplice saw him pour a few grains of some material into the glasses.

It didn't take long for the effects of the drug to start to show on Amin and Billy. At first, Amin just started to feel tired. Then Billy giggled at a drag queen holding court in the bar. He couldn't stop, even when she threatened to choke him with her feathery pink boa.

As sophisticated as Amin was, he would never assume that anyone would spike his drink. When he started to feel woozy, Amin tried to get up, but fell off the chair. The boys around him started to laugh. It didn't take Ben and his friend long to come up and pick up Billy and Amin. They made some minor apologies to the boys around them saying that their friends once again had too much to drink. Billy and Amin were literally unable to resist anything that was happening—they really weren't able to discern what exactly was going on.

Ben and the older man walked the two younger men out of the bar and turned the corner. Their car was parked on a dark side street, and nobody thought anything other than just a couple of gay guys that had too much to drink and a couple of older gay men who were there to help them.

When they were placed in the car, Ben securely bound their wrists with twine. The other man started the car and drove into the night. It was only about eleven o'clock when they left, but they were headed toward the east – the private area where the club had its play parties in West Virginia would be deserted right now, and they could do what ever they wanted with the two men. It didn't take them long to get on the interstate and be on their way.

Meanwhile, back at the house, Daniel was starting to get worried. He came down and woke Colin up. Colin, in turn, went down to Dominic's room and woke him up. It was a little after eleven, and all three of the men thought that Amin and Billy should be home by now. Dominic tried to call Amin's cell phone but got no answer. As they were trying to get their wits about them, Colin attempted to calm Daniel. He wasn't having much success in that area. Dominic said that Billy and Amin might have stopped off for a drink or something to eat, but there was an edge in his voice as well.

It didn't take long that night for Derek and Al to get up, join the group and get worried about Billy and Amin. Daniel was just about to get hysterical when Colin suggested that they go over to the Short North and see what was going on. The five men got into the Cherokee and quickly drove over. They looked in at the closed bookstore and then stopped in at the coffee shop. After that, they went to the bar located on that same street. Colin knew a couple of the waiters there and tried to track one down to see if they had seen Billy—none of the waiters would have known Amin. The first two boys said that they hadn't seen Billy in a long time. Finally, there was one waiter who said that Billy was there with a really hot man with dark hair and complexion. He also added that they had too much to drink and had to be helped out of the bar by two older 'friends' of theirs. The waiter had never seen the older guys before.

It didn't take any of the men long to realize what had happened that night. Dominic just assumed that someone had tampered with Billy and Amin's drinks because Amin rarely, if ever, over indulged in alcohol. Daniel became more frantic. Colin suggested a trip to the police station. When they got there, everyone, including Dominic went in. Colin explained what was going on and handed the sergeant the card that the detective had given him when he first came down here. The men were politely told that there was nothing that the police could do until the two men had been gone a little longer than a couple of hours. No matter how much Daniel tried to explain that Billy's life was in danger, the sergeant remained steadfast in his reply—they should come back tomorrow and deal with the detective.

When they got into the car, Daniel started to cry softly. Dominic, while just as worried, realized that he had to keep his cool in this matter. He would be the one who would manage to get Amin and Billy out of danger, and he couldn't risk not having his full wits about him. They drove home.

"Where do you think that they would take them?" Dominic asked.

"Does the club have any places around here?" Colin added.

All eyes were on Daniel, since he was the source of all information about this leather club. At first, he didn't realize that he was being asked questions that required answers. It took him a few minutes to respond quietly, "I don't know."

"Daniel, has this club ever had a meeting around here?" Al asked.

"No, not here. The closest was West Virginia," he answered.

"How far is West Virginia from here?" Dominic asked.

"The border is about two hours away," Derek replied.

"Do you remember where in West Virginia they met?" Colin asked Daniel.

Again, it took Daniel a long time to respond. It was as if he was in slow motion tonight. Finally he said, "I think that I could find it."

"Well then, you're coming with me," Dominic said.

"I'm coming along as well," Colin added.

"No, I don't want you to be involved," Dominic quickly responded.

"Colin, no. Don't go!" Derek said.

"I'm going with you guys. You're going to need more than just the two of you. Look at Daniel, he's not going to be worth much help there."

"Well, if you're going, I'm going," Derek said.

"No, we all can't go!" Colin said emphatically.

"OK. But I have a better idea. You let Daniel and I go together. You guys stay here and we'll call you when we have the place or at least the directions, and you can come and help us," Dominic said.

Dominic stopped by his room and got some guns and flashlights for the trip. He didn't let Daniel know that he had guns. The two men said goodbye to Colin, Derek, and Al and drove off into the night. They drove in silence, even though both of them were nervous, worried about their respective lovers. Daniel kept checking his cell phone, hoping that it was all a bad dream and that Billy and Amin were back at home.

Back at the house, Derek made a pot of coffee—it was apparent that no one was going to get any sleep tonight. Colin called into his administrative assistant and left a message that he would be out of the office for a couple of days. The three of them gathered around the kitchen table and waited for a call from either Daniel or Dominic. Colin was secretly holding onto the hope that Amin and or Billy would call, and this would all be a big misunderstanding.

"Do you think that Billy is in danger?" Al asked.

"I'm not sure. They could be just trying to frighten him. I doubt seriously that they are as sick as Brandy was," Colin replied.

"I'm not sure that we can count on that," Derek added.

"I'm not so sure either. I just wish that the police would have listened to us when we went down there the first time, this could all have been avoided," Colin said. "I can't believe that they would just let Billy be in danger."

"Well Colin, not defending them, but they really didn't have a lot to go on. Daniel heard these mysterious inquiries about Billy and he was all caught up in that stupid secret leather thing," Derek said, trying to calm Colin down a little, before he managed to get himself into some state. "And we can't expect the police to just go out and arrest people because they seem mysterious."

"There is the law against making terroristic threats," Al added.

"I guess that you guys are right. There is a law but we really didn't have any hard and fast evidence that these guys were up to no good. Maybe we should have just taken care of it ourselves, with Dominic's help."

"No, I don't think that would have been very effective. I am a priest and you are a hospital administrator, Al is studying to be a therapist or counselor. The last thing that we need is being involved in some sort of Mafia thuginess," Derek said. "I really don't approve of Dominic, although he is a really nice guy."

"If it's any consolation, Derek, I don't approve of what Dominic does either; it gives me the creeps. That's why he and I haven't been so close over the years."

"Then why involve him now?" Derek asked.

"Because I thought that the situation was beyond our fixing, and I really expected the police to act just like they did."

"You're too close to Billy, Colin. You have to start distancing yourself from him. We shouldn't be involved in this—it should have been over back in Pittsburgh. You should have left him and Daniel work this out on their own," Derek said. As soon as he said it, he realized that he had hurt Colin's feelings. He reached over and pulled his lover to him. "I'm sorry Colin, that was unfair."

As the three lovers managed to make themselves comfortable while waiting for the inevitable phone call, Dominic and Daniel had turned off the main road and were traveling down a small country road that lead to the turn off for the camp ground. They found it with very little difficulty even though it was black as pitch out in the country. They made their way up the winding little dirt road until they came to the locked gate. Obviously, if the two men had brought Amin and Billy here, they had a key to the place. Dominic assessed the situation quickly.

"Well Daniel, it looks like we might walk from here. Is it far?"

"Maybe a little under a mile."

"That's not too far. I have flashlights, but let's try not to use them. Our main goal is to surprise the two men or manage to get Billy and Amin without even waking the other two up."

Dominic and Daniel got out of the car and walked around the gate, climbing over an old fence. After a few minutes, Dominic asked Daniel if he could use a gun, handing him one of the guns that he had in his jacket. They then walked on in silence. It didn't take them too long to get to Ben's parked car. They knew that somebody was here—they hoped that it was the two men with Amin and Billy. They just didn't see anyone moving around. Of course, it was the middle of the night – about four in the morning to be exact.

"Dominic, do you think that we should call Colin and let them know that we're here?" Daniel whispered.

"If we can do it quietly—the slightest noise will sound like a gunshot out here tonight."

Daniel pulled out his cell phone. Miraculously it worked. He dialed Colin's number and was shocked when Derek answered.

"Derek, this is Daniel. We're at the camp, and it looks like someone is here. I can't talk long but I wanted to give you the directions to this place just in case."

Derek wrote the directions down. He told Daniel that they would be leaving shortly to get closer to where they were. And yes, all three of them were coming. No one was going to be left at home to wonder. If Billy and Amin were not there and were on their own, they both had keys to the house. They would leave them a note to call someone if and when they got home. Derek then hung up the phone.

None of the men should have driven that night—they were all dead tired. Al volunteered to drive Colin's jeep to the turn off for the campsite. Maybe there was some place there that they could wait until they received further word from Dominic or Daniel. Colin rode up front with Al, Derek in the back seat. As they pulled onto the interstate, Derek started to quietly pray to himself. It had been some time since he had prayed. It was marvelously comforting for him. It didn't take him too long to be fast asleep. Colin looked back and threw a coat over him—smiling at his lover as he did so, and they placing his hand on his other lover's knee as they continued to drive on in silence.

Dominic and Daniel had managed to get as close to a cabin as they dared. They did see Ben and the other man asleep, but there was no sign of Billy or Amin. They thought that they would look around for a little while, trying to find their lovers. They still hoped that they could manage to get out of here without a confrontation. It would be dawn soon, and they would be able to see around the camp a little better. The two men in the cabin had to be tired, they couldn't have had much sleep tonight – Dominic and Daniel hoped that they would sleep in tomorrow, giving them a chance to find Billy and Amin.

It seemed that Colin, Derek, and Al made it to the turn off in record time. Of course, in the middle of the night there isn't much to impede you as you travel down a four lane divided highway. They managed to find a fast food restaurant, so they took their phones and went it. It was dawn. They knew that they couldn't call Dominic or Daniel—the noise might alert the other two men to their presence. They simply had to be patient and wait—and eat greasy food.

Chapter 17

Dominic and Daniel were crouching in thickets as dawn broke. They had searched the entire area and couldn't find either Amin or Billy. They realized that they would just have to take things into their own hands, and confront the two men. It wasn't going to be too difficult, two older men sound asleep couldn't pose much of a threat, and Dominic and Daniel had weapons.

They were literally creeping up to the cabin. They had decided that they would burst in, taking the two men by surprise and would over power them. They had found some leather restraints in the campground and would make sure that the two older men couldn't get loose. Then they would do whatever it took to make them lead them to their lovers.

Dominic and Daniel both couldn't believe how tired and how stiff they felt when they got to the cabin door. It was hard pulling an all-nighter, especially an all-nighter out in the cold woods. They stopped at the door. Dominic counted to three and then burst through the front door. He jumped on Ben while Daniel jumped on the older man – the four of them wrestled for a bit, but Dominic and Daniel had the advantage and soon had the two of them restrained to the post in the room.

"What the fuck are you two doing here?" Ben screamed.

"You cannot believe how much trouble you two are going to be in," the older man added.

Without thinking, Dominic hit the older man across the face with his pistol, saying, "Shut up! You two are going to listen to us now. First, where are our lovers?"

Ben kicked Daniel hard in the balls. He fell over. Dominic reacted quickly and found rope to secure their feet and legs as well as their hands. He placed the barrel of his gun right between Ben's eyes. "You do that again, and it will be your last act."

"You hurt us and you will never find your lovers. At least not alive," the older man said.

Dominic sat down on the edge of the bed. He quietly looked at the two older men. "Are either of you leather bottoms?" He asked.

They both laughed, and said, almost in unison, "No way. Do you think that a bottom could do what we do? Why do you ask that?"

"Because, if you two don't cooperate with me, and quickly, you're going to see what true pain is – I will hurt you in ways that you never thought possible and you will beg me to kill you. Am I making myself clear, here?"

"I doubt that you could do too much to us son. You are too pretty for that," the older man said.

Without even hesitating, Dominic shot Ben's toe off. Ben started to scream—blood rushing from his foot. "Don't worry—it will clot before you loose too much blood."

"You better watch what you're doing boy, you don't know who you're dealing with here," the older of the two men said.

Ben was crying out in pain – there was a lot of blood on the floor, but like Dominic said, it quit long before he was in any danger from loosing too much blood. Daniel was clearly out of his element here. He had no idea that Dominic would be so intense. It was almost like an SM scene gone bad.

"Now, who is going to tell me where my lover and Billy are?" Dominic asked.

"That's just it, boy—neither one of us is gong to tell you anything!" Ben said, straining at his restraints.

Dominic very quietly went over to the corner and picked up a four-foot length of two by four. He came back to the two men and smacked Ben's knee hard. Ben cried out in pain once again.

"Look guys, I have all day to wait and I can keep this up as long as you like. The simple fact is that I'm not leaving here without our friends. I can work each one of you over until you may never walk again."

"How do we know that you won't kill us if we tell you?" The older man asked.

"Well, you'll have to trust me on that one. What you *do* know is that I *will* kill you if you don't tell me."

Daniel was clearly uncomfortable with what was going on. He loved Billy but he had never seen anyone be so brutal with another person, especially when that brutality had nothing to do with some sort of scene. He tapped Dominic on the shoulder and asked him to go outside.

"Dominic, do you have to be so horrible to those guys?"

"Daniel, don't you think that they have harmed our lovers in some way? They tracked Billy down and then drugged him and Amin and brought them out here. I can't imagine what those two boys feel right now, and I'm not sure that they are OK. If they harmed my Amin, I don't care what happens to them."

"This isn't how I handle things, Dominic. Why don't we just call the police and have them come up here."

"Look Daniel, you stay out here. Call Colin; tell him where we are. I'll go back in and take care of things."

As Dominic went back into the cabin, Daniel started walking away. He wanted to cry; he was certain that Billy was dead and that he was going to go to prison for what was happening now. When he got to the edge of the clearing, he pulled out his phone and called Colin.

"Colin, this is Daniel."

"Did you find Billy and Amin?"

"No, we didn't. But we did find Ben and his friend here. So Billy and Amin must be close by."

"Are you two all right?"

"Yes—Ben and the other guy are tied up. Dominic is torturing them."

"Torturing them?"

"Yes Colin, torturing them. He is being brutal to them. Can you come up here, please?"

Colin agreed. Actually he was relieved to be heading toward them. He wrote down the directions quickly and gathered up Al and Derek.

"Are you sure that he said that Dominic was torturing them?" Derek asked.

"Yes."

"He just doesn't seem the type to do that. He's so gentle around the house."

"Derek, the man makes his living with people who do harm to other people. I love him dearly, but he is quite capable of hurting those two men. I just hope that we can get there before he kills them."

"Colin, come on. He wouldn't kill them, would he?"

"I'm not sure."

While the three of them were winding their way up the hill in West Virginia, Dominic was still terrorizing Ben and his friend. Daniel was sitting on the ground outside the cabin with his head in his hands. Every time that he heard Ben cry out, he winced, as if in pain himself.

In another clearing, away from the camp, Billy and Amin were tied to poles, out in the open. They were naked and hanging limply from the poles. They had been beaten with a bullwhip and both men were had dried blood on their backs. They had gags in their mouths, and neither one of them was moving at all.

Back in the cabin, Dominic was continuing his work on Ben and the older man. He was determined to get to information out of them. Ben eventually passed out from the pain. Dominic then looked at the older man.

"I guess that it's your turn now."

"If you let me go – untie these restraints. I'll tell you where the boys are."

"And I guess that I'm supposed to believe you?"

"What am I going to do? I'm an old man – I can't outrun you down the hill. But now you have Ben here unable to tell you anything. If you do the same to me, your lover and his friend could die."

"So, you're willing to sacrifice Ben so you can possibly get away?"

"It's every man for himself. That's what I always said."

Dominic looked him closely in the eyes. The older man felt like a steel blue laser was being used on him. Dominic really didn't trust him, but it was worth a chance. Ben was pretty much useless, at least for a while. Maybe the guy could at least tell them where Billy and Amin were. He's right, he could never get down off of this hill faster than he and Daniel could.

As Dominic was untying the older man, Colin and his lovers had reached the gate. Derek picked the lock and they continued to drive up to the campsite. They saw Daniel sitting on the ground with his head in his hands.

"Oh no. They must have really hurt Billy," Al said.

"Come on guys, keep your wits about you," Colin cautioned the men.

In the cabin, the older man stood before Dominic who had his gun aimed directly at his head. "If you go to the edge of the clearing, there's a path. Take the path about five hundred yards. You'll come to another clearing. Billy and the other man are there."

Dominic hit the man across the face with his gun. The older man fell down and Dominic kicked him hard in the balls before running out of the cabin. Seeing the household there, he called out for them to follow him. It didn't take long for them to find Billy and Amin. The five men rushed to their friends and untied them. Both of the men were alive. They had been severely beaten, and they were suffering the effects of exposure to the cold.

"Quick, take off your jackets. Let's get them covered and back to the cabin. We have to build a fire or something," Colin said.

They carried them back to the other clearing. Derek suggested putting them in the jeep, since it was already warm and they could turn the heat up. They did just that.

"We have to get them to a hospital," Al said.

"I know. We have to call the police as well," Derek added.

Dominic and Daniel were just standing by the side of the car. They looked like they were in shock. Neither of them knew what to do with their lovers. Finally, Derek took control of the situation.

"Al, you call the police. Colin, you take Dominic and Daniel down to the nearest hospital with you and have them see to Billy and Amin."

"Are you nuts? Those two guys are here somewhere," Colin said, clearly not leaving his lovers here with Ben and the other man somewhere.

Dominic ran into the cabin. Ben was still there—still tied to the pole, but conscious. He was hurt but not fatally so. The older man was gone—just as Dominic suspected. He came back out.

"Colin, you take Daniel and Derek down with you. Al and I will stay here and call the police. There's no danger now."

Colin, along with Daniel and Derek got into the jeep with Billy and Al. Neither of the two boys stirred at all – Daniel sat in the back, cradling Billy in his arms. Derek kept holding Amin's hand. The jeep drove down the hill faster than was probably safe. When they got to the gate, they saw Dominic's car but the other car that was in the camp when they arrived was missing.

Just as they got to the small country hospital, the sheriff was pulling into the campsite. He was what you would think that a rural West Virginia sheriff would look like, heavy set with an ill fitting uniform; cigar hanging out of his mouth.

"What's up here, boys? Did y'all call for police?"

"Yes officer, we did. The man in the cabin and his friend kidnapped two of our friends. They were held here and beaten and kept outside, naked, all night long."

"Where are your friends?"

"A couple of other friends have taken them down the mountain to the hospital."

"Would you mind telling me what in the hell a bunch of city boys are doing up on this mountain in the winter?"

"Sir, we wouldn't have come here if the man in the cabin hadn't taken our friends here."

"Well, let's go have a little look see at the man in the cabin, okey-dokey boys?"

"Yes Sir," was Dominic's only reply.

When they got into the cabin, Ben was screaming. "Arrest that man! Look what he has done to me! He shot me, and pistol whipped me, and he beat me with a two by four!"

The large sheriff looked directly at Dominic. He didn't think that the pretty young man in front of him had it in him to do any kind of malfeasance to anyone, let alone an older man like the one that was tied to the pole. "Did you do what the man is saying, boy?" He asked, addressing Dominic.

"Sir, he kidnapped our friends and beat them with a bull whip!"

"Well now boy, that remains to be seen, right? What I have here is his word against yours. So, we'll just have to go on down the hill and find these alleged victims. Now, did I hear you say that there were two people involved in this crime?"

"Yes Sir, the other one must have gotten away."

"Well mister, did you have a friend here last night with you?" The sheriff asked Ben.

"I don't know what he's talking about—I've been here alone the whole time."

"What about this boy's friends. Did you whop 'um?"

"Do you see anybody but us here, officer?"

"All right—I've just about had enough of this. I don't believe any of you. I'm callin' my deputy. We're goin' to take all three of ya down the hill. First off, we're goin' to try to find these alleged kidnap victims. I'll call MaryAnn over at the hospital. She'll tell me if anyone came in lookin' like the boy said that they looked."

The sheriff went out to his car and radioed his deputy who made it up the hill in record time. Ben went in the car with the sheriff, in handcuffs. Al and Dominic were with the deputy, both of them in handcuffs. They were to drive down to the hospital and see if the nurse that the sheriff mentioned had seen anybody with the injuries that Dominic had told the sheriff about.

When they got to the hospital, Derek and Colin were standing in the small waiting room. The sheriff came in with Ben and turned him over to one of the nurses to tend his wounds. The deputy came in shortly there after—Dominic and Al in handcuffs behind him.

"Take those cuffs off of them! They didn't do anything wrong!" Colin shouted at the sheriff.

For all of his big city sophistication, Dominic knew that was the wrong thing to do. He had played it very cool and very respectful with the sheriff.

"You just have a sit down there, boy," the sheriff said to Colin.

"Don't you dare call me boy—take those handcuffs off of those two right now or I'll sue your fat ass from here to kingdom come. Do you understand me?"

"Now you just calm down a minute there. We're goin' to get to the end of this, don't you worry. If they didn't do anything, we will let them go."

A nurse in her mid-fifties approached the group. She was slightly overweight and had somehow managed to dye her hair coal black. She had ruby red lipstick on and the whitest starched uniform and nurses cap that Colin had ever seen. "Why hello there sheriff, we certainly are busy today," she said to the sheriff.

"Sorry to bother you MaryAnn, but these boys have some crazy story that their friends were kidnapped and bull whipped up on the mountain. Have you seen someone with those kind of injuries?"

"Yes sheriff, I have. They are in the other room. They've both been beaten pretty bad. One of them is awake and doing OK—the other one is in bad shape."

"Which one is in bad shape?" Dominic cried out.

"The one that's not Billy," was all she said.

"Sheriff, you have to let me out of these, I have to go to him."

"What in the sam hill. . ." the sheriff began. MaryAnn pulled on his sleeve and whispered in his ear, "They're gay Earl, the one's boyfriend is in there with him. This one must be the other's boyfriend."

"Well, I never in all my life," the sheriff declared. "Can the one that's awake talk to me?"

"Yes. Come with me," MaryAnn answered.

The sheriff went in and asked Daniel to leave. Daniel began to protest, but decided that it was for the best. He went out to join his friends. When he saw Daniel and Al in handcuffs he panicked, thinking that they would all be under arrest. The sheriff was very kind to Billy asking him what had happened. Billy started at the beginning, telling the sheriff about the murder in Pittsburgh and Brandy Mantune. He then went on to tell him about what Daniel had heard during the leather club meetings, and finished up by referring to the store surveillance tape back in Columbus. Then he began the saga of what happened, saying one minute they were in a bar and the next thing that he and Amin knew was that they were tied up to a pole and being whipped. MaryAnn came in and told the sheriff that he should leave the boy alone for a while; he needed some rest.

"Can I see the other boy?" The sheriff asked.

"Yes, but he's really bad, Earl, come on," she said.

MaryAnn led the sheriff into the next room. Amin was lying on the table—lots of blankets around him and an IV in his hand. He was pale. "I don't know if he's going to make it, Earl," MaryAnn said.

"This is a damned shame MaryAnn. What in the hell do you think was going on up there?"

"Well Earl, I don't rightly know. I do think that all of these boys are involved in a little perversion."

"MaryAnn, they're queer, of course they're involved in perversion."

"No Earl, I mean that they tie each other up and hit each other. That stuff that they call S-A-D-O-M-A-S-O-C-H-I-S-M."

"You don't say! Here in good old West Virginia?"

"You got to talk to the one that was yellin' at you when you came in. He seems to know all about it. And he's a big hospital administrator over in Columbus."

"There's a hospital administrator involved in this thing?"

"Yes, and the other one's a priest."

"MaryAnn I told you about them Catholics a long time ago."

"No Earl, he's not Catholic—he's one of them uppity Episcopalians."

"Well, now isn't that rich? You wouldn't think of those prissy-assed people involved in this kind of thing."

The sheriff decided to call the Columbus police and confirm that Billy and Colin had made a report to them about Ben and his friend. He quickly got a hold of the detective who not only read him his initial notes, but also the report that was filed when no one could find Billy or Amin. He made a picture out of the surveillance tape and FAXed it to the hospital. Ben was easily recognized on the picture, the other man was a little obscured.

"Well Johnny, you better get those cuffs off of those two. Their story pans out," the sheriff said to the deputy.

"Can I go see my lover, sheriff?" Dominic asked as he rushed by him.

Dominic became ashen when he saw Amin lying there on the bed. He ran over, fell to his knees and started kissing his hand. It was so cold. There was a monitor above the bed and the little beeps indicated an irregular heartbeat. MaryAnn came in and stood beside Dominic without saying anything for a few minutes. She put her hand on his shoulder.

"How is he?" Dominic asked.

"He's pretty bad, son. He was out in the cold for too long. The other boy was younger, and I think probably a little more used to the cold."

"He and I live in Chicago—it gets plenty cold there," Dominic replied. Then he remembered how Amin suffered through Chicago's bitter winters. "Is he going to be all right?"

"I'm not sure. The other man out there wants to transfer him and Billy to a hospital in Columbus. We're waiting for an ambulance to come."

"That's probably a good idea. I'll stay here with him until they come."

MaryAnn patted him on the shoulder. She really didn't understand homosexuality, and she didn't have any kind of sympathy for SM, but she knew what love was, and she was sure that this man loved his friend in the bed there. She reverted to the nurse/mother image that she was famous for in these parts.

Out in the other room, the doctor had finished with Ben. The sheriff was instructing the deputy to take him down to the jail cell. Kidnapping is a pretty serious charge and the man would be sent back to Columbus for trial and hopefully prison. After the sheriff finished telling Colin, Derek, Al, Daniel, and Dominic not to leave the state of Ohio when they got back, the ambulance arrived. It could hold both Billy and Amin, along with Daniel and Dominic. They crawled into the back of the ambulance with an attending nurse and were off. Colin and Derek took their car back while Al drove Daniel's car.

Chapter 18

Colin pulled out onto the interstate, having driven through the Deliverance-style landscape in shell-shocked silence for almost an hour. He said nothing. Derek just sat and stared out of the window; only his tight lips and clenched fists betrayed his mounting fury. It was Derek who opened the conversation. "Colin, what do you think happened back there?"

"I'm not too sure. They wouldn't let me talk to Billy for too long. I know that he was beaten and left out in the cold."

"Ben didn't look too good when they brought him in. What do you think that Dominic did to him?"

"Again, we didn't talk too much either. He was pretty worried about Amin. I imagine that he went crazy with the guy, after all, he was holding his lover against his will."

"That kind of violence scares me, I don't know how you deal with your cousin and his lifestyle."

"Well Derek, I can tell you that it bothers me as well, but in this case, I'm going to give him a little leeway. After all, Billy's and Amin's lives were in danger."

"Colin, there is no way that violence like that can be tolerated. What Dominic did was wrong."

"Derek, would you please give me a break here—I haven't slept. My cousin had to rescue our roommate and his own lover from maniacs, and I am just not in the mood to discuss the philosophy behind the actions. I probably would have done the same thing if you were in that situation."

"That even scares me more, Colin. I can't abide violence—using brute force to get your way. It goes against my whole perception of the world. What would happen if I did something to you that Dominic felt was an insult—would I then be subject to his violence?"

"Derek, I think that you know me by now. I'm not going to have you harmed because we had a disagreement. I just think that the situation here was justified. Can we drop this right now?"

Colin's eyes were locked straight ahead and his jaw was set.

Derek had pushed an issue a little too far at the moment. It just wasn't the right time. Derek, in the passenger's seat turned his head to face the window and watch the passing scenery, not that there was much of it—mostly trees, and boring trees at that. The ride home was going to be quiet. Colin silently fumed, as he wondered why Derek always had to make issues out of things, and why he had to make them always at the wrong time. In a couple of days he would be willing to commiserate with Derek, even possibly agree with him. He just didn't know what Derek expected of him. Did he want Colin to push Dominic out of his life? Did he expect Colin to make it all have not happened at all?

In the ambulance, the nurse was tending to Billy and Amin. Both of the men had IVs running and both were on oxygen. They were under warming blankets. Daniel sat beside Billy, holding his hand. Every once in a while they would whisper at each other, or kiss. Dominic was kneeling beside the gurney on which Amin lay. Amin seemed to be coming around. He opened his eyes, but didn't say a word.

"Hey, he's awake!" Dominic told the nurse.

"Hi babe, how are you?" He said in a quieter voice to Amin as he bent over to kiss his lover on the lips.

Amin could hardly speak. He had been through a lot. He whispered, "I love you."

Dominic then did something that he rarely, if ever, did. He began to cry. "I'm so sorry I didn't get there before he hurt you. I love you, Amin."

Amin squeezed Dominic's hand and then Dominic laid his head on Amin's chest. The nurse tended to Amin, adjusting the heat of the blankets, and changing the rate of the IV. He took Amin's blood pressure and his pulse. The two lovers just held onto each other. Dominic stroked Amin's head, pushing his straight, dark hair back. Amin held onto Dominic's hand and whispered, "Don't leave me, Dom."

Dominic couldn't stop crying. He could barely talk, but he held onto Amin tightly. Then, the unthinkable happened. Amin's heart just stopped. And then his breathing stopped. There was no dramatic turn of events, the man just died. The nurse was the first to realize it from the monitor. He began CPR immediately, pushing Dominic out of the way.

"What' happening?" Was all that Dominic could say.

The nurse worked on Amin for over ten minutes. He was doing everything that was possible. Billy and Daniel just watched in horrified silence from the other side of the ambulance. Dominic sat on the floor, looking terrified; like he couldn't believe that this was happening. The truth was that he thought that he had fallen asleep and he was dreaming this. When the nurse reached the conclusion that further action was futile, he stopped. He turned to Dominic and said, "I'm so sorry."

"NO! It can't be. God, please help him. Please make this stop. Oh God, I can't go on without him—please, God, please......... I'll do anything. NO!" And then Dominic, now realizing that it wasn't a dream, sobbed uncontrollably on the floor of the ambulance. The nurse and Daniel tried to console him, but he just continued to sob and beat his fists on the floor. After about fifteen minutes, he reached up and held Amin's head in his arms. "I'm so sorry babe—it's my fault that you're like this. I can't believe that I caused this, please…please…please…come back to me." When Amin's lifeless body offered no response, Dominic began to pray, "God, I know that I've done wrong, please, let him come back, I'll change, I promise, please." And then, Dominic started to sob again.

The ambulance made it to the hospital before either Colin and Derek or Al. Billy was admitted right away, but really only for observation. Amin was declared dead on arrival. The physicians were trying to calm Dominic down, and offered to give him a sedative, but they couldn't make him listen to them.

Colin and Derek arrived around the same time that Al did. They all walked into the emergency entrance together, a little world worn, but glad that the nightmare was over. When they inquired about their friends, the nurse told them Billy's room and went to get the doctor to tell them about Amin.

Dominic came out of the room and saw his cousin. Colin realized that something was wrong and ran over and grabbed him. Dominic was crying so hard that he was beginning to shake. He couldn't talk, he could no longer see, and he could barely breathe. As he collapsed to the floor, Colin called for assistance. They carried Dominic back into an examining room. It was there that Colin found out that Amin had died. The cause of death was listed as exposure—he just never rebounded from it. He instructed the physician to sedate his cousin, and to give him some sedatives for when they got home.

"I don't think it's a great idea to have a lot of pills around the house. He's in bad shape," the physician told Colin.

"Don't worry, I'll keep them."

When it looked like the medicine was taking effect, Colin left his cousin and went out into the waiting area. He walked over to Derek and Al and told them quietly that Amin had died because of his treatment at the hands of Ben and his accomplice. Al assumed the look that all priests had when confronted with the death of someone dear to them; a look as hard as that of an Old Testament patriarch. Derek began to cry softly. Both Colin and Al put their arms around him. He turned to Colin and whispered in his ear, "I'm so sorry—I feel so guilty now."

"Don't let it bother you. Let's go and see Billy and Daniel."

The three men went up to Billy's room. The reunion, which should have been a happy occasion, was tempered by Amin's death. They all hugged and kissed. It was Billy who spoke first, "How's Dominic?"

"He's not good Billy, but we will try to help him get through this," Colin answered.

"From what I saw, I don't think that you will be able to do anything that will help him right now," Billy continued.

"Billy, you forget. We're gay men. For my whole life, my friends have died because someone beat them up because they were gay, or they died of AIDS because they were gay. As upset as I am right now, and as much as I share Dominic's pain, there's a part of me that is just resigned to accepting it."

The nurse came in and gave Billy a sedative. When he was asleep, Daniel joined the other three as they were leaving. Colin went into the emergency examining room and picked up his cousin, carrying him out to the car. Dominic was so deeply sedated that he didn't even move.

When they got home, Colin went upstairs and put Dominic in his bed. Dominic, whenever he would wake up, would be surrounded by Colin, Derek, and Al. For that matter, Daniel would be invited to join them if he wanted. When he was sure that Dominic was still soundly asleep, Colin went downstairs. He needed something to eat, and he needed a bath, and then he needed to sleep.

The police were at the door when he reached to bottom of the stairs. Colin invited them into the living room and called the rest of the household there. They were told that Ben would be tried for murder, in addition to the other charges. All of them would probably be required to testify. When asked about the other, older man, they said that Ben would not tell them who he was. As a matter of fact, Ben denied that anyone was with him—even though the evidence gathered proved that there was a second man. The picture from the bookstore surveillance tape was not clear enough to make any kind of identification. The police were dusting the whole campground in West Virginia for fingerprints.

Colin inquired as to how to inform Amin's biological family of his death. The police had already done that. It seems that his family had disowned him long ago. Their Islamic belief would not permit them to even come and grieve his death.

Billy came home the next day. It was a somber homecoming. Dominic had regained a little of his composure, but was still helped along by the pills that Colin insisted that he take. It had been Amin's wish to be cremated, and when the coroner was finished with the body, Colin made sure that his wishes were carried out. Dominic was still in no shape to make any kind of decisions. Over the next couple of weeks, the six men in the house stayed pretty much together. Most of them didn't do much with their jobs, although Colin did do some work at home and Derek did preside at the liturgy on Sundays.

Dominic eventually came around, just a little. At first, it was only enough to discuss a memorial service for Amin. Derek offered to find an Islamic clergyman to perform it, but Dominic insisted that it should be someone who knew, and even loved, the beautiful Syrian man. He didn't want a stranger to bury his lover. Dominic asked if Derek could put something together. He agreed. Colin called a few of the friends that Dom and Amin had in Chicago and told them about what happened and gave them the date of the memorial, which would be in two more weeks.

One night, when they were all around the table, Colin asked his cousin, "Why don't you consider staying here?"

"Thanks Colin, but this house is bursting at the seems already."

"Don't be silly, Dom. We have room," Derek said.

Colin couldn't believe what a turnaround Derek had made regarding Dominic. They were really getting closer.

"I do like being around you guys."

"Well stay then," Colin said.

"You would get tired of me. Besides, I have a home in Chicago."

"Well, keep it and go there on vacation."

"I don't think I could bear going there right now—or even going to Chicago."

"OK, then it's settled, you'll stay here," Colin said, pushing the issue.

"Colin, I would get in the way. I'm the only unmarried one. You know what they say about an unmarried woman in the house with a married couple. . ."

"Hey," Billy interjected, "the house next door is for sale. It's not quite as big as this one, but it's nice. The two guys who lived there have moved away."

Dominic looked at Colin. Neither one of them had to exchange words. They could communicate on a higher level. The deal was made without a single word being spoken. By the time that the memorial took place, Dominic was in much better shape. Friends from Chicago came. The memorial was beautiful, with Derek doing his best to structure it around Amin's life and culture. It was definitely somber. Dominic cried a lot. The entire household cried. But after it was over, he seemed to change a little.

It didn't take long for the house next door to be acquired by Dominic. When you're paying cash for something, a lot of time is excised from the process. While the closing hadn't happened, at least the date had been set. He decided that he would leave his place in Chicago, as is. He would buy new furniture. He still couldn't bear to be confronted by the life that he shared with Amin. Colin was right, a new beginning would help him get back into the swing of things.

Dominic even had his lawyer suggest someone 'friendly' to be his counsel during the upcoming trial. Everybody was coached on his testimony. The trial wouldn't be for some time, but the household was prepared—this time. The police didn't seem to make any connection with Dominic's Mafia underworld connections. Or, if they did, they simply didn't press the issue.

The days that passed since the memorial seemed to be ones of quiet healing. The men gathered regularly. They shared meals and, sometimes, drinks. Dogs were walked. Gossip was exchanged. Sometimes, old stories from long ago would be remembered and shared with the small somber community.

It had been some time since any of the men had sex. Oh, of course Daniel and Billy were having sex, but Colin, Derek, Al, and Dominic hadn't had any sex since the incident. It was the longest that Colin had gone without sex since his days in the seminary. All the men were masturbating regularly, but no one talked about *that*. Colin knew that Derek and Al were sexually attracted to Dominic. You didn't wake up in a bed with four hard-ons in the morning and not notice that there was definitely desire there. He decided to arrange for a little playtime in the basement.

One Saturday afternoon, he told Derek and Al to get the basement ready. And to be prepared for a fun time that night. After dinner, Colin started to serve drinks to them and his cousin. Around nine o'clock, while Dominic was in the bathroom, he told Derek and Al to go downstairs and get ready. He had already gone downstairs and made sure that the *room* was ready – there were candles all around, and his favorite 'toys' were placed out, all in order. When Dominic came downstairs, he asked where Derek and Al had disappeared.

"They're in the basement, Dom."

"Oh, I guess that it's time for me to go to bed."

"That's not what I had in mind."

"Oh come on, Colin. You're not an Eskimo, you don't have to offer me your spouses for the night to be hospitable."

"I wasn't offering them to you—I was offering to play with them and you, cousin."

Dominic couldn't believe it. Years ago, Colin had sworn that he would never be intimate with Dominic again. Dominic also didn't know if he was ready for a step like this.

"I'm not sure, Colin. I don't know if I can."

"I'm told that it's like riding a bike. And I'm also told that it's like muscles—you either use them, or you loose them."

"Your lovers may not like me."

"Oh, they like you Dom. But, even if they didn't, they would still have to do what I told them down there."

"I haven't seen your dungeon, yet."

"Don't you think that it's about time?"

Dominic came across the room and grabbed Colin, kissing him passionately on the mouth. The two men stood there for the longest time, kissing and caressing. Dominic let out a sigh that signaled his return to life.

"We better get down there soon, or my lovers will fall asleep. They sometimes don't have a long attention span."

"After you, cousin. You can lead me."

When the two men entered the dungeon, Derek and Al were already naked and on their knees. Dominic held back a bit, waiting to take his cue from Colin. It didn't take long for the two naked boys to have their hands tied behind their backs, and to both be sucking Colin and Dominic.

After a little while, Colin put Al up on the cross, and had Derek kneel down in front of Al's naked body. As Colin started to flog Al, he instructed Derek to keep Al's cock in his mouth. Soon, Dominic took over as Colin stood behind him, massaging his back while he continued to flog Al. After about fifteen minutes, Colin stopped Dom and took a butt-plug and stuck it up Al's ass. He reached around and put tit clamps on Al's nipples and then fixed a leather hood on Al's head. Derek still had Al's cock in his mouth.

"Boy, get up and get over here," Dominic said to Derek.

Derek got up and went over to Dominic, who fixed his hands to the wall hooks and then proceeded to flog him relentlessly. Derek was writhing in pain, but enjoying every minute of it.

Colin undid the restraints and ripped Al from the cross. He forced the man to his knees, unzipped his jeans again, and waved his piss-swollen cock in front of Al's mouth. Al opened his mouth and Colin began to piss in it. "Don't you dare spill one drop boy." Al obeyed, soon reaching the point where he was gagging in order to keep swallowing Colin's piss. When Dom took Derek off the wall, he pushed him to the ground and pissed all over him. It was a simple courtesy to his cousin to only piss on, and not in, his lover.

Colin grabbed Al's coal black, thick hair and yanked him to his feet. He shoved Al roughly into the sling with Colin assuming his position at the foot and Dom at the head. Dom put his cock in Al's mouth, while Derek knelt behind Dom and ate his ass. Colin put K-Y jelly all over his hand and slowly put first one, then two, and then three fingers up Al's ass. With perfect patience, he continued until his whole hand had disappeared in Al's ass. When it was in there, Colin didn't move, but Al had arrived at a place that he had never been—he had never felt this way before, and he couldn't believe that he was not experiencing some sort of spiritual ecstasy. Colin very slowly started to move his hand, in and out, almost in a punching mode. Al groaned with delight. This went on for some time, until Colin decided that Al had enough. He gently pulled his hand out of Al's ass and wiped it on a towel.

Colin pointed to the bench on the other side of the room – he bent Al over one side while Dom bent Derek over the other—they fucked the two boys roughly, staring deeply into each other's eyes. It didn't take them long to cum. When they had, they pulled out and instructed the boys to get themselves off. Derek and Al knelt on the floor masturbating, while Dom and Colin kissed deeply. The two boys came quickly. They were instructed to lick it up, which they did.

When it was over, no one said a word. They went to separate bathrooms to clean up—Derek and Al going to one while Colin and Dominic went to another. When they had washed off, they all managed to meet at the bed at the same time. Again, in total silence, they climbed into the bed. The cuddled with each other, Colin holding Dominic while Al and Derek held onto each other. Colin managed to take his free arm, and reach over Dominic to touch his lovers in their embrace.

In the morning, Derek got up first. He showered again and got ready to go over to the church. He couldn't believe the mixed feelings he was having. Sex last night had been great—and he totally enjoyed Dominic. The hardest thing for him today would be to preside at the liturgy. He wondered if his partners would make it there.

Al was the next one to get up. He went downstairs and started breakfast. He knew that Derek never ate on Sunday mornings. While he was puttering around the kitchen, Dom and Colin woke up and made love to each other, tenderly. It was not surprising that sex was so intense. Colin thought about how the death of a friend or loved one always made the people left behind so horny—as if, by having sex, they would affirm their own life. What was so surprising was how that one sexual encounter affected all four of the men. It would take them some time to sort through what had happened, and their feelings about it. Not one of them mentioned how they were feeling that this lifestyle and their sexual proclivities managed to get Billy in danger and Amin killed. The scene the night before in the dungeon was an exorcism—a proof to them that their desires were still there and were, at least in their minds, OK.

A Boner Book

Chapter 19

Derek couldn't believe that the date for Millicent's consecration as bishop, and consequently, her becoming his boss, was upon them. They were all going to go to the church for the ceremony. He was playing such a minor role in the whole thing, but he would be there to support his long time friend and colleague. The ceremony was to begin late in the afternoon, and it would be in Columbus. Millicent had forgone the use of her own cathedral because the city in which it was located was involved in a major racial incident. She was pointedly making a statement that she did not approve of the city's policy or record on minorities. Anyway, that gave Derek a little time to get some work done around the parish.

He was meeting with two women who were going to have their commitment ceremony in two weeks in his church. He enjoyed these kinds of things; it always reminded him of his and Colin's ceremony. That was a joyous day for him. He even was willing to compromise in situations like this when it came to the liturgy and what could or should be done. This couple even went to all of the trouble to put the announcement of their upcoming 'nuptials' in the local paper. Derek was surprised that the conservative paper even agreed to publish it.

By noon, Derek returned to the house to get ready for the consecration. Everyone in the house was already showered, shaved, and dressed, sitting quietly in the library and were looking very much like an advertisement for Episcopalian Weekly. He glanced in, and without saying a word, jumped into the shower. He was ready in a flash.

Since Millicent had chosen not to use her own cathedral, the ceremony was taking place in the Catholic Cathedral in Columbus. When they got to the church, Derek separated from the clan and went to the area designated for the clergy. The five other men walked up the few steps to the large wooden door and entered the church. They made a resplendent procession as they found their way down the nave of the church, five very good looking and very well-dressed men under the age of forty five. It was an unusual occurrence at a church service, outside of the clergy, which always contains a significant number of men.

The bells signaled the beginning of the liturgy, with trumpets announcing that the incense bearer had reached the front of the church. All eyes turned toward the door. The procession itself took almost forty minutes to make its way through the church and up to the altar. Derek passed his lovers and friends with only a small raise of the eyebrow to indicate that he knew them. When Millicent passed by, there wasn't even that small sign of recognition.

After the liturgy, the clergy and the people were invited to a large reception at the local convention center. That required finding the car and driving over a few blocks and then parking the car again. By the time that they were all walking into the convention center, Derek had just about had enough of the festivities. He, and his group, were starved. Of course, when they finally got into the area, there was food and drink aplenty.

Millicent had already arrived and was seated in a very large wooden chair on a dais in the back of the room. The Episcopal and American flags surrounded her and her coat of arms hung above her head. To Colin it was very much reminiscent of a throne and throne room. He chose not to use that moment to mention it to Derek.

Billy felt very much out of place here, as did Daniel. They weren't really church people, and, before their interaction with Derek, wouldn't have known the bishop from a hockey player. They stayed close together with the others. Al was somewhat used to these things, and Colin, as a Rector's wife, had been to many of them before. He glanced over at Dominic, who seemed to be taking it all in. For all of Dominic's association with the Mafia underground, he maintained a public life that very much involved with hanging around Catholic bishops and cardinals. But of course, he lived in Chicago, and this was Columbus, so he felt he would just have to do with an Episcopalian bishop. Although, it *was* hard for him to see a woman in those robes up there—he wasn't sure if he was opposed to women clergy or not, but he had never been this close to them before.

Derek went up to the throne and made what Colin could only call an obeisance. When he came back down to his group, Colin smiled at him.

"Did you vow perfect obedience and lifelong loyalty to Her Majesty?" Colin asked, joking.

"Don't get smart. But do you know what she said to me?"

"No, what?" Al asked.

"She said, I see that you and your group got yourself in the papers again."

"Maybe she was just kidding you, Derek," Colin said and reached out to put his arm around Derek's shoulders, and then decided that this wasn't the proper thing to do at this time, in this place.

"Who knows? I just know that I've about had enough of church politics for today. Maybe I should have another drink."

While Derek found his way to the bar, Colin and Dominic went up to Millicent to wish her well. They had to wait in line, behind a rather significant number of old Episcopalian ladies who were doing the same thing.

When they got to Millicent, Colin reached out to shake her hand. She kind of limply handed him her hand, but not in the manner of handshaking. For a minute, he thought that she wanted him to kiss her hand or her ring. He put that thought out of his mind. It must have been a holdover from his Catholic roots.

"Millicent, congratulations. I hope that this new turn in your ministry is rewarding for you."

"Thank you, Colin. I'm sure that it will if you can manage not to get my old friend and priest in trouble too much more."

"Millicent, have you met my cousin, Dominic from Chicago?"

"Oh no, I haven't. A pleasure. Are you visiting Columbus, Dominic?" She asked, leaning over to hear above the crowd.

"I was. But now I think that I might just move here for a while."

"Oh sorry, now I remember. You recently lost your friend."

"Oh no, ma'am. I lost my lover."

"Yes. What do you do? Have you found work in Columbus?" She asked.

"Dominic, I think we've taken enough of Millicent's time. Again Millicent, accept our congratulations to you on this wonderful day. You will have to come over soon for dinner."

Dominic and Colin retreated into the crowd, looking for Derek and Al. They spotted them and snaked their way around the people to get to them. Derek looked as if he had found the bar, all right, but he didn't seem to have found any food.

"Hey, little one, you better take it a little easy. You don't want to get blotto in front of all of your peers, not to mention your boss," Colin teased.

"Well then, maybe we should just leave."

Colin looked at Al who raised his eyebrows an inch. They found Billy and Daniel and made their way out of the building and into their cars. Al suggested that they find a quiet place to eat, but Derek wanted to go home and change his clothes first. They all thought that was a great idea, getting comfortable before going out to eat.

When they got home, Colin called the fancy local gay restaurant and made reservations. Surprisingly, he didn't have a hard time. They were seated there in a few minutes. Derek's mood improved immensely once he was free of his clerical collar, even though Colin's locked chain reminded him that he would never be his own master again. It was refreshing to be with his friends in a gay environment. The food was good that night, and the wine flowed freely. When they finally got back home, everyone was exhausted except Billy. Derek had to get up early to preside tomorrow, so Colin suggested a family night of movies and snacks. The weather had turned miserable and cold, so all of the men thought that it was a great idea.

"Who wants to go to the video store with me?" Billy?" Colin asked. Billy was always the one who accompanied him before.

"I think that I will go," Derek replied. Everyone was surprised. Derek never volunteered to do these things.

"Come on then, get your coat," Colin said.

The two men went back out to the video store. As they were walking around the aisles, looking for a couple of movies to entertain six men with very differing tastes, Derek started to tease his lover. "I hope that I didn't stop a quicky that you had planned with that boy."

"Derek, stop it! You know that I haven't done that."

"Do you miss it?"

"OK, sometimes I look at him and miss the challenge of an older man bringing a younger man off. But, do you really want to know what I miss the most?"

"What?"

"You."

"Me? I'm always here. You can't miss me—I'm always giving you grief about something."

"That's just it Derek. You have been giving me a lot of grief. And that's a part of marriage, I know that. But sometimes you have to balance the ledger—give me a little of your old self."

"I *have* been crabby lately, I know that. I just feel trapped by being a priest."

"Then stop being an active priest. Take a sabbatical. Rest. Figure out what you want to do."

"Colin?"

"Yes?"

"I love you."

"Thank you. I love you to."

They found a movie and checked out as Derek piled the counter with sodas, popcorn, and candy. On the way home, Derek started playing with Colin's crotch. When they pulled into the driveway, he leaned over and unzipped Colin's jeans, and proceeded to give him a blow job, right there in the driveway. As Colin came in his mouth, Derek grabbed his own cock and came quickly after.

"What did I do to deserve that?" Colin asked.

"Did you like it?"

"Wasn't that apparent?"

"Let's just say I'm settling old accounts and balancing ledgers."

Colin lightly smacked his lover upside his head. They opened the door and went into the kitchen to prepare the necessary things for a cold winter's night's television movie watching.

Chapter 20

Dominic finally had the closing on the house next door to Colin's. Now there were six attractive gay men living in the two houses. Colin secretly hoped that soon there would be a seventh; sure that Dominic would find someone to share his bed. They decided to do something unusual. They erected a big wooden privacy fence around the two back yards and placed an extension of that between the two houses. The fence only went around the periphery of the combined yards and didn't separate them. Finocchio loved it. He could romp freely without being on a leash. He loved it even more when Dominic came home one day with a German shepherd puppy named Dracul.

Billy kept his job at the bookstore, but now cleaned both the house that he lived in and Dominic's house. Sometimes, when he was cleaning Dominic's house, he and Dom would have sex. Billy loved it. He didn't think that it was cheating; after all, Dominic had become family. And he knew that Daniel sometimes had sex with Colin because Daniel told him that one night in a fit of guilt. He and Daniel worked that one out and now, everyone seemed to be happy about it.

Al continued his studies. He had pretty much decided that he wouldn't seek active ministry in the Episcopal church—it was one thing to be a gay Episcopalian, or even a Catholic, for that matter, it was entirely different when you are a priest. Derek seemed to be having trouble with it. Al was happy, studying, and working part time, and living with his two lovers.

Colin's consulting business started to take off. Ohio was ripe for someone as well versed in managed care as Colin was. He even managed to get a couple of consultants to work with him. Derek knew that his goal was to start a business that would require him to only be peripherally involved, but to be able to support himself. If things continued going as they were now, that might become a reality. Colin's true desire in life was to be a writer—if he could find some enterprise that required very little effort on his part, maybe he could realize that goal.

Dominic became a frequent guest at dinner, and would often cook for the others. He really didn't have to work because he had a significant amount of money stashed away. He was enjoying his semi-retirement. His 'bosses' back home were being particularly patient with him. He and Colin had sex from time to time, and the distance that had grown between them disappeared.

Derek still struggled with the emptiness that he felt in his ministry. He justified staying by telling himself that he would serve the gay community. He wanted to make St. Peter's a gay church, but he knew that he would loose the few straight people that were there. He continued to hold commitment ceremonies, and was in his office preparing for one between two young men when the phone rang.

"Hello, St. Peter's"

"Hello Derek, this is Millicent."

"Well hello there, Bishop. We haven't talked in some time."

"I know. I keep telling myself that I have to make some time for my old friends, and to limit the amount of work that I'm doing but I never seem to get there."

"What can I do for you, Millicent?"

"I'm glad that you asked that. I know that this is going to be hard, and I know that you will disagree with it, but I would like you to stop performing gay commitment ceremonies at St. Peter's. Diocesan canons actually don't provide for it, you know."

The silence on the other end of the phone was deafening. Derek was trying to take his time to form a response. "Millicent, I know that you don't agree with that. When we were in Pittsburgh, you often would perform them."

"Derek, we aren't in Pittsburgh, and I'm not a priest anymore. I'm a bishop."

"Does being a bishop mean that you can't minister to people anymore?"

"That's not fair Derek. You know that I have to walk a thin line. The conservatives will kill me with this."

"Millicent, do you mean the same conservatives that are opposed to women's ordination and to divorce? Are those the conservatives that you are afraid of, or are you only afraid of the one's that are opposed to gay priests and gay people in general?"

"Derek, you're really not being fair here. Please stop performing them."

"And if I don't?"

"I'll have to take the appropriate actions."

"Millicent, we all have to do what we have to do. Look, I'd really like to talk, but I'm really busy today. Perhaps we can discuss things further in the future."

They hung up amicably enough. Derek walked through his office and into the church. He sat in one of the chancel choir stalls for a few minutes, and then knelt. It had been so long since he had privately prayed. Interestingly enough, he started by telling God how thankful he was for Colin and Al. How much being with them, though tedious at times, had enriched his life. Then he prayed for Amin asking for peace and for Dominic, asking for healing. After he told God how much he really liked Billy and Daniel he then asked God why he no longer felt the same zeal he had felt when he was ordained. Was this what Christ experienced on the cross when He asked, 'My God, My God, why have You abandoned me?' Finally, he prayed that God would be present next week when he officiated at Jim and Bernie's wedding. Not at their commitment ceremony, at their wedding.

He got up and went to get his coat. He left the church and his office early that day. Billy was at the bookstore and no one was home in the house except Finocchio. Derek went into the kitchen and opened several cookbooks. Tonight was going to be a feast. And after that feast, he and his lovers, and, if they were inclined, their friends were going to go down to the basement for a really hot scene. Derek wanted Colin to take him to the same edge that he had watched when he fisted Al. And after that scene, they were all going to sleep together.

Finocchio was happy. Derek, his favorite person in the house, was spending the afternoon in the kitchen, his favorite room in the house. And Derek was happily sharing small bits and pieces of food with him as he was preparing dinner. There couldn't have been a happier puppy. Billy, for some reason, got home early that day – before the rest of the household.

"Billy, do you want to come to a dungeon party tonight?" Derek asked.

"Where, and who is going to be there?"

"In the basement, silly. And we will. You and Daniel should come, and maybe, Dominic will come too."

"Are you feeling all right, Derek?" Billy asked.

"Of course I feel all right, why are you asking that?"

"Of all the years that I have known you, you have never once asked me to have sex with you and/or Colin. Are you sure?"

"Of course I'm sure. You want to help me fix dinner?"

"Derek, now you are scaring me. Have you suddenly started taking anti-depressants or something?"

Derek picked up a spatula and smacked Billy on the shoulder. Billy retaliated by picking up a dough ball and throwing it at Derek. For one brief moment it looked like there might be an old-fashioned food fight in the kitchen. But Derek, as playful as he was today, was still a gay man, and it was his dough that was being bandied about. Not even playfulness would interfere with his dinner. He and Billy prepared the dinner together, and then went upstairs to get ready for their night. At one point, he grabbed Derek by the shoulders and shook him, saying loudly, "Whoever you are, please come out—give us Derek back."

When Colin came home that night, he was greeted by Derek, who kissed him passionately as he came through the door. Then Billy did the same. Colin looked a little perplexed, but decided not to press the issue.

All six men were at the table for dinner that night. They laughed and told stories and ate a really wonderful meal. Billy made coffee for them—real coffee, not decaffeinated as per Derek's instructions. Later on, they all ended up in the basement and Derek plans for the evening came to life. The six of them were down there for several hours, and groans and expressions of ecstasy could be heard throughout the house.

That night, none of them thought of the Dark Knights of St. Germain, or of the upcoming trial. Derek didn't think of Millicent or of how to be or not to be a priest. They all only thought of the moment at hand, and the effects were exhausting for all of them. Later, gathered around the kitchen table like sisters, they shared a desert that Derek had purposely not told them about at dinner.

When they finally calmed down, they went to their beds, Dominic joining Daniel and Billy for the night. As Colin and Derek locked up the downstairs and started up the steps, Colin asked, "What did I do to deserve that?"

"Just balancing the books, lover, just balancing the books."

There was only a tiny night light on. Everyone was asleep upstairs as Finocchio and Dracul curled up together on the kitchen floor. They were sure that the men would be in this room tomorrow for food---they knew when their masters spent time downstairs, they always had a lot of food the next morning. And they always shared.

About the Author

Chuck Williams was born in Pennsylvania in the 1950s. He attended university and several graduate schools, never quite deciding on what he wanted to do with his life. Introduced to leather in the late seventies, he became one of those men dressed completely in black leather, hidden by the shadows in leather  bars across the world. While reading and writing are two of his passions, he actually makes his living in the scientific community. He currently lives in Pittsburgh with his lover, Michael, and a very, very bad dog.

www.ingramcontent.com/pod-product-compliance
Lightning Source LLC
Chambersburg PA
CBHW071226260626
47162CB00004B/1434